P9-BYX-200

"If I can help, you know I will," Richard said gently.

He sounded sincere. Melissa was tempted to confide in him, to share her troubles, but she held back. "Thanks, Mr. McNeil."

"You used to call me Richard."

"And you used to call me brat."

He chuckled. "Not to your face."

She smiled for the first time in days. "No, not to my face, but I knew you disapproved of me."

Turning in his seat to face her, he said, "I never disapproved of you, Melissa, but sometimes I disapproved of the things you did."

She couldn't meet his gaze. "The wildest Hamilton kid has a news flash for you, Richard. Recently I've done a lot of things you wouldn't approve of. Making mistakes seems to have become my forte."

"People can change, Melissa. It's not too late."

"I hope you're right."

DAVIS LANDING:
Nothing is stronger than a family's love

Books by Patricia Davids

Love Inspired

His Bundle of Love #334
Love Thine Enemy #354
Prodigal Daughter #372

PATRICIA DAVIDS

was born and raised in the farm and ranch country of central Kansas. As a tomboy with four brothers, Pat spent an idyllic childhood where horses, softball, church activities and books formed the foundations of her rich imagination. Today Pat works as an R.N. in the NICU, spoils her grandkids and tries to find time to write down the stories roaming around in her head. She is president of her local RWA chapter and believes that helping new writers learn the craft is the best way to repay the people who helped her. After seven years of writing, she sold her first book to Steeple Hill in June of 2004. Dreams do come true—as long as you chase after them with hard work, determination and faith.

PATRICIA DAVIDS

PRODIGAL
DAUGHTER

Steeple
Hill®

Published by Steeple Hill Books™

If you purchased this book without a cover you should be aware that this book is stolen property. It was reported as "unsold and destroyed" to the publisher, and neither the author nor the publisher has received any payment for this "stripped book."

Special thanks and acknowledgment are given to
Patricia Davids for her contribution to the
Davis Landing miniseries.

To my daughter, Kathy, with all my love.
Thank you for the precious gifts of Joshua and Shantel
and for being my best friend.

STEEPLE HILL BOOKS

Steeple
Hill®

ISBN-13: 978-0-373-87404-0
ISBN-10:   0-373-87404-9

PRODIGAL DAUGHTER

Copyright © 2006 by Harlequin Books S.A.

All rights reserved. Except for use in any review, the reproduction or utilization of this work in whole or in part in any form by any electronic, mechanical or other means, now known or hereafter invented, including xerography, photocopying and recording, or in any information storage or retrieval system, is forbidden without the written permission of the editorial office, Steeple Hill Books, 233 Broadway, New York, NY 10279 U.S.A.

All characters in this book have no existence outside the imagination of the author and have no relation whatsoever to anyone bearing the same name or names. They are not even distantly inspired by any individual known or unknown to the author, and all incidents are pure invention.

This edition published by arrangement with Steeple Hill Books.

® and TM are trademarks of Steeple Hill Books, used under license. Trademarks indicated with ® are registered in the United States Patent and Trademark Office, the Canadian Trade Marks Office and in other countries.

www.SteepleHill.com

Printed in U.S.A.

"There is hope for your future," declares the Lord,
"and your children will return to their own territory."
—*Jeremiah* 31:17

The Hamiltons of Davis Landing

Nora McCarthy – m – Wallace Hamilton

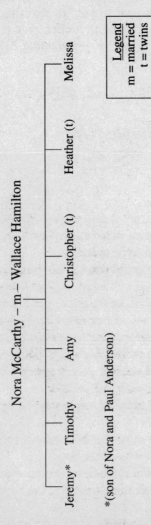

Jeremy*   Timothy   Amy   Christopher (t)   Heather (t)   Melissa

*(son of Nora and Paul Anderson)

Legend
m = married
t = twins

1. Heather's story: BUTTERFLY SUMMER by Arlene James   (LI #356, 7/06)
2. Chris's story: BY HER SIDE by Kathryn Springer   (LI #360, 8/06)
3. Amy's story: THE FAMILY MAN by Irene Hannon   (LI #364, 9/06)
4. Tim's story: THE HAMILTON HEIR by Valerie Hansen   (LI #368, 10/06)
5. Melissa's story: PRODIGAL DAUGHTER by Patricia Davids   (LI #372, 11/06)
6. Jeremy's story: CHRISTMAS HOMECOMING by Lenora Worth   (LI #376, 12/06)

Chapter One

"Y'all be careful up there, sugar." The elderly woman's rich Tennessee drawl slid off each word the way warm honey slips off a spoon.

Richard McNeil glanced down at his great-aunt. At eighty-eight, Lettie was still a spry lady who faced life with wit, humor and an abiding love for her family. Today, she wore her favorite pale blue cotton print dress and a thin blue sweater tied over her slightly stooped shoulders. Her snow-white hair was styled into old-fashioned waves, and she had a death grip on the side of the rickety folding ladder he stood on.

"I'll be fine, Aunt Lettie, but maybe you should move away…just in case."

She scurried to the other side of the camel back sofa with amazing speed for a woman her age.

"If you fall, you're likely to lie on this floor until the cows come home 'cause there's no way I can be picking up a man your size."

Richard replaced the burned-out light in the high

ceiling fan and stepped down with a sigh of relief. He had lost a good twenty pounds after his doctor took him to task, but his six-foot-two-inch frame still carried plenty of muscle. The antique stepladder his great-aunt had pulled from the depths of her hall closet for the occasion had creaked and groaned, but held—this time. He would see that she had it replaced with a sturdy new one before the next bulb died.

"And the Lord said, 'Let there be light,' and there was. Thank you, my boy. That surely will help these old eyes to see the Good Book again."

"My pleasure, Aunt Lettie. Is there anything else I can do while I'm here?" He resisted the urge to glance at his watch. He enjoyed Wednesday afternoons with Aunt Lettie, but each time he came to visit, she would find excuse after excuse to keep him from leaving. She was lonely, he understood that. More than once over the years, he had tried to convince her to move into a retirement home where she would have the company of folks her own age.

Lettie stubbornly refused to budge from the apartment over the shop in downtown Hickory Mills, Tennessee, that had once belonged to her and her husband. Their furniture store had long since closed and the space downstairs had been sold and converted into a shoe store, but Lettie wouldn't budge from her home. She always said that she had lived here for seventy years and the only way she was leaving was in a pine box. When it came to stubbornness, the good Lord had broken the mold after He fashioned Lettie Corbet McNeil.

Glancing around, Richard had to admit her home was cozy. The high, molded plaster ceilings made the place feel spacious while the tall arched windows with white lace curtains let in plenty of sunshine. Their gleaming panes were reflected in the polished surface of the cherrywood sideboard with its brass candlesticks and artful arrangement of old china plates and figurines. All of her antique furnishings shone with loving care, from the gilt-and-black-lacquer Regency writing desk in the corner to the massive oak pedestal dinning table with its ball-and-claw feet.

His great-aunt was, he realized, very like the things she owned—a beautifully preserved part of a bygone era.

The tiny woman laid a hand on her cheek and tapped gently as she considered what needed repairs. "Let me see. The front door gets to squeaking something awful when the humidity is high."

"I oiled it when I first came today."

"Oh, that's right, you did. Well, I reckon that's all there is, but you don't have to run off, do you?"

"I need to get back to the office."

"Don't you work half days on Wednesday?"

"Things have been a bit hectic lately. I have some paperwork to catch up on."

"Your papa would be so proud to see you in that fancy place over in Davis Landing. You might have come from humble beginnings in Hickory Mills, but you've made your mark in the world. And that house of yours! My, my! It's big enough to hold a dozen young'uns."

"It feels crowded these days."

"How is your sister getting along? Such a sad thing, her house catching fire like that. 'Twas a blessing from the Lord that no one got hurt."

"Angela and Dave are doing okay. The girls are adjusting, but it's been hard on them. The renovations on their house should be done in another two months. I was glad to give them a place to stay, but I do miss my peace and quiet. Angela said to tell you that she and the girls will be over to visit on Saturday, as usual." He picked up his suit jacket from where it lay folded over the arm of the sofa and slipped it on.

"I'll be glad for their company, that's for sure. I reckon having those two little girls living with you is making you wish you had a family of your own. It's long past time you settled down and got married. You're not getting any younger, you know."

"I'm thirty-four. You make it sound like I've got one foot in the grave."

She set her hands on her hips and leaned back to look up at him. "Like I said—long past time."

He leaned down and kissed her wrinkled cheek. "I'll get married when I find a girl who can bake a pecan pie as good as yours and not before."

"Oh, go on! Flattery will get you nowhere."

"I was hoping it would get me one more piece of pie."

"You take the rest of it home with you for those girls. And mind you don't go eatin' more than your share on the way."

Ten minutes later, Richard sat behind the wheel of his black Mercedes in downtown Hickory Mills and switched on his windshield wipers as drizzle began to fall from the leaden sky. If only he could have left Lettie's fifteen minutes earlier, he would have missed the jam of traffic that accompanied the local dockworkers getting off shift and the arrival of the afternoon bus. Visiting with Lettie was always a high point in his week, but he hated wasting time in traffic.

As he waited impatiently behind two taxis loading baggage and passengers, he noticed the Collin's Drugstore across the street was for sale.

The tall window cases were bare except for the red-and-white For Sale sign taped to the glass. He had worked there as a stock boy through most of high school. Several other stores on the block had closed over the past few years and hadn't found new owners. Graffiti marred the cinder block wall beside the bus station and trash littered the alley. It was sad to see his old neighborhood going downhill.

His cell phone rang and interrupted his musing. He pulled it from his pocket. His secretary's quiet voice claimed his attention.

"Mr. Delaney is here to see you, sir."

"Delaney? He doesn't have an appointment today."

"I told him that, sir." Margaret Woodrow's voice dropped even lower. "He insists you said it would be all right to just drop by any old time and add a codicil to his will."

Richard chuckled. "He probably wants to disinherit his ungrateful nephew again. Or is he adding him back? I can't remember—he's changed it so many times. All right, Margaret. I'm still in Hickory Mills. I'll be there in about twenty minutes. If he can wait, I'll see him."

He tucked his cell phone back in his pocket. The line of traffic hadn't moved, but at least the other lane was clear. He checked in his rearview mirror before pulling out and stopped short. Was that Melissa Hamilton leaving the bus station?

Turning his head to get a better view, he saw that he was right. She walked past him to the street corner. There, she set down her black duffel bag and raised a hand to sweep her long blond hair back over her shoulder.

She certainly was as lovely as ever. The overcast sky couldn't dim the taffy and honey brightness of her thick hair. It flowed in rippling waves almost to the center of her back. She was dressed in a flared skirt with big yellow sunflowers on a red background and a yellow blouse with short puff sleeves. Over her arms she had draped a red shawl with a yellow fringe. Pulling the flimsy shawl up to cover her shoulders, she shivered and turned her back to the wind. The late-October air definitely had a chill in it. As he watched her, the rain began in earnest. She glanced up, then lifted her shawl to cover her head.

Richard frowned. What on earth was the daughter of Wallace Hamilton doing coming into town on the bus?

Not that it mattered how she got here. The important thing was that she was home again. Wallace and Nora had both been worried sick about their youngest child. Melissa had left town with her boyfriend months ago and no one had heard from her since. That in itself was bad enough, but to disappear when her father was seriously ill seemed totally selfish. As the baby of the Hamilton family, she had always been overindulged and spoiled, but this time she had gone too far.

Wallace's publishing firm, Hamilton Media, was one of Richard's most important clients, but more than that, Wallace and Nora were his friends. He knew what a strain Wallace's leukemia and bone marrow transplant had put on the man and his family. That Melissa had run off without a word hadn't set well with Richard and a lot of other people.

He had always hoped the lovable but wayward girl would come around and grow up into a responsible adult like the rest of the Hamilton kids, but maybe he had been wrong about her.

He watched as she tried to hail a cab, but the taxis in line already had fares. She looked around as if she didn't know what to do next. Suddenly, he was struck by how fragile and bewildered she looked.

Vivacious and flirty was the way he would have described Melissa five months ago. She had always used her charm, including batting those big brown eyes at men, in order to get her way. Now, the woman shivering on the corner simply looked tired and lost.

It only took him a moment to decide what to do next. It wasn't the first time he'd helped Melissa Hamilton out of a jam and it wasn't likely to be the last. He pulled out around the taxis and stopped at the corner in front of her. He pressed the electric button and the passenger-side window slid open. He leaned across the seat and called out. "Melissa, do you need a ride?"

Melissa jumped, startled by the sound of someone calling her name. She clutched her shawl more tightly and leaned down to look in the car that had pulled up beside her. Her father's attorney sat behind the wheel of a shiny, black sedan.

She had to admit that Richard McNeil looked decidedly handsome in his charcoal-gray tailored suit and white button-down dress shirt minus a tie. It had always amazed her how such a big man could wear his clothes so well. With his rugged good looks, black hair and fabulous bright blue eyes, it wasn't surprising that she had suffered a crush on him in her teenage years. Maybe she still harbored a trace of it, she thought, if she were being honest with herself.

Of all the people who knew her family, why did Richard McNeil have to be the one to see her slinking back into town?

"Mr. McNeil, what are you doing here?"

"It looks like I'm offering you a lift."

She hesitated, not sure what to do next. Glancing around, she saw that no empty taxi had appeared. Waiting for one would only prolong the inevitable encounter with her sister. She took a step toward the car. "I hate to be any trouble."

"It's no trouble. I'm on my way back to my office, but I can drop you off at your home if you like."

She bit her lip and hesitated, then said, "Could you drop me off at my sister Amy's instead?"

"Sure thing. Hop in before you get any wetter." A flurry of raindrops accompanied his words.

"All right. If you're sure it isn't any trouble." She picked up her bag, opened the door and slid into the front seat. Instantly, she was engulfed by the masculine scent of his aftershave, the smell of leather upholstery and the aroma of…was that pecan pie? Her stomach did a flip-flop.

"I can put your bag in the trunk," he offered.

"No, this is fine. Thank you." She wrapped her arms around her duffel and held it tightly in her lap, hoping to hide her pregnancy for a little while longer. At five months she wasn't showing much, but it wouldn't be long before even her full skirt and baggy peasant blouse wouldn't conceal how far Wallace Hamilton's youngest daughter had fallen.

She asked, "Do I smell pecan pie?"

"You do. My great-aunt Lettie sent one home with me. It's on the back seat if you'd like a piece."

"No thanks." Her stomach rumbled. She couldn't tell if she was hungry or if she was going to be sick again. Either way, the thought of pie wasn't appealing. She rolled her window down an inch to let in some fresh air.

"Are you okay?" he asked, looking at her in concern.

"I'm fine." She wasn't, but she didn't want to elaborate on the cause. She glanced at him out of the corner of her eye, then looked straight ahead. As he pulled out into traffic, Melissa rode in silence. After all, what could she say to defend the way she had acted? She glanced at him several more times. His face was set in stern lines, making her feel nervous and ill at ease even though she had known the man since she was eleven.

Face it, Melissa. It's time to stop procrastinating. She knew why he was upset. "Have you seen my dad lately?"

"I was about to ask you the same thing." He didn't quite mask the edge of sarcasm in his voice.

Here it was, the conversation she had been dreading. "I know what I did wasn't right, but I do love my father, and I am worried about him."

"You have a funny way of showing it."

"Yeah, well things aren't always what they seem, are they?" He wouldn't understand the irrational panic that swept over her at the very thought of seeing her father in a hospital bed. No one understood it. Least of all Melissa herself.

She had tried to visit when her father was first

admitted. She had made it to the wide doorway of the stark glass-and-steel building, but she couldn't make herself go in. She had wanted to—but she couldn't. If she had needed to save her own life by walking through those doors, she would have died on the sidewalk. Instead, she had run to Dean and kept on running. Until now.

Richard cast her a puzzled glance. Instead of the scolding she expected, he said, "I'm sorry if I sound like I'm condemning you. Your parents and your brothers and sisters have been very worried about you."

"I know. How is Daddy?"

"He's back in the hospital, but he's doing a little better. They were able to find a bone marrow donor for him and it looks like the graft is working. He's had a few setbacks, including a nasty infection his doctors have been fighting, but your mother is hopeful that he'll make a full recovery."

"That's Mom. The family's eternal optimist."

"Your mother relies on her strong faith, Melissa. That's what has gotten her through this."

"People always give God credit for getting them through the bad times. Kind of funny, isn't it, when He gave them the bad times to start with." Melissa didn't try to conceal the bitterness in her words.

He cleared his throat once, then asked, "Are you back in town to stay or is this merely a visit?"

"I'm not sure." Besides her parents, she had three brothers and two sisters who would soon know about her condition. No doubt they were all angry with her for running away when their father was ill and the family was in such turmoil. For an instant, she considered getting out of the car and heading back to the bus station.

It would be easy to just ride away from the painful confrontations ahead of her, but her seldom-used common sense kicked in.

A hundred and twenty-four dollars was all she had left of the money her sister, Amy, had sent. It wouldn't last long. It certainly wouldn't be enough to get a place to live while she looked for a job.

"I take it things aren't going too well for you and…what is his name?"

"Dean Orton. No, things aren't going well for us."

That had to be the understatement of the century. She was twenty-three years old, single and pregnant. She had no money, no job and her baby's father was long gone.

It wasn't fair. All she had wanted was a life free of the expectations tied to being the daughter of Wallace Hamilton. She thought Dean would give her that life. She desperately wanted to love him and be loved in return. His dreams of making it big with his rock band had sounded exciting and exotic.

If he had been surprised by her sudden offer to travel on tour with him, he hid it well. Life on the road with Dean was a far cry from her family's successful publishing business and the strict Southern upbringing she had known.

Only Dean hadn't really loved her. All he wanted was a piece of the Hamilton fortune. When she realized that, she had been heartbroken. And she discovered that having morning sickness in a run-down motel on the outskirts of Detroit wasn't exotic at all.

"I'm sorry things didn't work out for the two of you," Richard said, turning on to Mill Road and heading toward the bridge that led to Davis Landing.

She scowled at him. "You don't sound sorry at all."

"Melissa, I've known you since you were a kid. I play golf with your dad, and your mother invites me to dinner. I'm a friend of the family, and that means *all* of the family. I care about you and your happiness." The rain had stopped and he turned off his wipers.

"I know," she admitted, turning to stare out the window. "Things are just so messed-up right now."

The sounds of the tires changed as the car rolled across the bridge spanning the Cumberland River as it snaked its way through the beautiful tree-covered hills of Tennessee. Upriver she could see the hills were ablaze with fall colors of gold and scarlet, but even their beauty didn't lift her spirits. Below her, Melissa watched two paddle wheelers moving with stately grace as they steamed past each other. Their stern paddles churned the gray river water into white latte foam behind them.

On board, their cargo of tourists hung over the pristine white wooden rails festooned with swags of red, white and blue as they enjoyed a trip back in time. The boats were from Nashville and Davis Landing was one of several stops on their itinerary. How many times as a child had she begged her father to take her on board one of them? No matter how many times he had relented and agreed, she had never tired of the ride. What she wouldn't give to go back to those carefree days.

Richard reached over and laid a hand on hers. "I, for one, am glad you decided to come back, Melissa. Your family needs you. I don't know how much you know about what's been going on since you left."

"I spoke with Amy not long ago. She sort of filled me in. I know that Jeremy is only our half brother." She cast Richard a sidelong glance. As the family attorney, had he been privy to that secret before the rest of them?

He said, "It came as a shock to everyone. Especially to Jeremy."

Another major understatement. "No kidding. Did you know that Mother was pregnant when she met Dad?"

"No, they never told me. It wasn't until your father became so ill that anyone knew. He'd accepted Jeremy as his own child. He told me keeping the secret was his decision. I think he knows now that it wasn't a very wise one."

The car left the bridge and entered the business district of Davis Landing. Old redbrick-fronted stores and black iron lampposts added to the town's quaint turn-of-the-century charm. Just ahead, she saw the three-story brick office building that housed her family's business, Hamilton Media. Both the *Davis Landing Dispatch* newspaper and the *Nashville Living* magazine had offices there.

Her great-grandfather had started the paper as a local weekly in the 1920s. Under the sound business hands of both her grandfather and then her father, the business had grown to a daily paper and now included a monthly lifestyle magazine that enjoyed tremendous success locally and across the region. Except for her brother, Chris, who had decided to become a cop, all of the Hamilton children had worked alongside their father in the family business.

"Amy said that Jeremy and Dad had a falling-out, that Jeremy quit." As the company's vice president, her oldest brother, Jeremy, had been her Dad's right-hand man and everyone assumed he would take over the company when the time came. Now what would happen? Would her brother, Tim, as second in line, step in to run both the paper and the magazine?

Richard nodded. "That's true. Apparently Jeremy and Tim had quite a fight about it. To make matters worse, the story was leaked to the *Observer*."

"I imagine they had a field day with that. The *Observer* loves a good scandal and they've been trying to put Hamilton Media out of business for years."

"A smear campaign won't accomplish that."

"You're our attorney. Why don't we sue them?"

"Because what they printed was true."

She waved aside his comment. "Oh, that's just a technicality."

"It's an important one in court. We were worried about how the news leak would affect your father, but he's holding up well."

"What about Mom? She must feel like her reputation is in shreds." Melissa knew exactly how that felt.

"Your mother's answer was that if people who didn't know her wanted to talk, she couldn't stop them. She said the only thing that matters is how she is living her life today—not what she did thirty-five years ago. She's kept her head high. Your mother is a true lady."

"Now I'm back to add to their troubles." Melissa wondered if she would be able to hold her head up when her condition became known.

"What's wrong, Melissa?"

"Nothing."

"I don't think that's true."

"Okay, it's not, but it's not something I can talk about right now."

"If I can help, you know I will," he said gently.

He sounded sincere. She was tempted to confide in him, to share her troubles, but she held back. "Thanks, Mr. McNeil."

"You used to call me Richard."

"And you used to call me a brat."

He chuckled. "Not to your face."

She smiled for the first time in days. "No, not to my face, but I knew you disapproved of me."

He stopped the car in front of the entrance to the Enclave, an upscale condominium not far from the downtown area. Turning in his seat to face her, he said, "I never disapproved of you, Melissa, but sometimes I disapproved of the things you did."

She couldn't meet his gaze. Instead, she looked up at the building where three of her siblings made their homes. "The wildest Hamilton kid has a news flash for you, Richard. Recently, I've done a lot of things you wouldn't approve of. Making mistakes seems to have become my forte."

"People can change, Melissa. It's not too late."

"I hope you're right."

"I know I am. Just take it one small step at a time. The Lord will carry your burdens for you if you let Him."

She chose not to offend him by offering an opinion on his beliefs. He was welcome to them; she just didn't share them anymore. She pushed open the door of his car and stepped out. Hefting her duffel bag over her shoulder, she leaned down and said, "Thanks for the lift, and I'd like to ask for one more favor."

"Certainly, if I can."

"Please don't tell my parents that you've seen me."

"Very well, but may I ask why?"

"I've got to make some decisions before I see them. But don't worry, I'll see them soon."

"All right. Take care of yourself, Melissa."

"I will. Goodbye."

As he drove away, Melissa felt as if her only friend were leaving her in front of the lion's den. Facing the building, she looked up at the six-story structure with renewed qualms about the wisdom of this move.

"The truth is, I don't have much in the way of options," she muttered.

She squared her shoulders and walked through the front doors. The uniform-clad guard on duty was one who knew her on sight. He nodded in her direction, then went back to reading the paper. The *Observer,* she noticed, not her family's paper, the *Dispatch.* Even burly security guards liked a little scandal, it seemed.

She took the elevator to the fourth floor and quickly found Amy's apartment. Standing in front of her sister's door, a dozen doubts flew through Melissa's mind. What if Amy wouldn't let her stay? What if she insisted on telling Mom and Dad about the baby? What if none of the family wanted her back?

"One small step at a time, Melissa. That's all you have to do," she whispered, remembering Richard's words.

Taking a deep breath to quell the butterflies in her stomach, she raised her hand and knocked on the door.

Chapter Two

Melissa rapped on the door again, then waited, fighting down the urge to run. She was the bad penny, returning to bring more trouble to her already overburdened family. Maybe this hadn't been such a good idea. She took a step back, but the door opened before she could vanish.

Amy stood framed in the doorway, looking at first startled, then genuinely pleased. She grinned and Melissa knew she had made the right decision after all. She took a step toward Amy and found herself enveloped in a warm and welcoming hug. She cherished the feeling as she returned her sister's embrace.

A second later, Amy drew away but kept her hands on Melissa's shoulders. Her hug was immediately followed by a firm shake. "It's about time. Where have you been? When you didn't show up after I sent you money, I thought you'd changed your mind."

"I did change my mind. About a dozen times, and then I changed it back again. I wasn't sure anyone would want to see me after the way I took off."

"Of course we want you home. Everyone has been worried sick about you, Mom most of all."

"How is she?"

"Holding up. You know Mom. She's the Rock of Gibraltar in our family."

"She is that." Melissa's voice dropped to a whisper. "And Daddy, how is he?"

"He's had a hard time of it. He's lost weight and he's pale but he's as stubborn and determined as ever. It hurt him when you ran off with Dean."

"You don't have to tell me that Daddy doesn't like Dean. I think that was partly the reason I started going out with him."

"Now that you're back, you should go see Dad."

Shaking her head, Melissa looked away. "I can't. Not yet."

Amy took Melissa's hand. "Look at me, standing here scolding you instead of inviting you in. Come on, I have some people I want you to meet."

Melissa hesitated. "I'm sorry. I didn't know you had company. I should have called first. I'm not feeling up to meeting strangers."

"These people aren't strangers. They're going to be part of your family, too."

Amy pulled Melissa inside and steered her toward the condo's spacious kitchen. A man and a young boy rose to their feet beside the table strewn with pieces of a jigsaw puzzle.

"Bryan, Dylan, I'd like you to meet my sister Melissa. Melissa, this is Bryan Healey and his son Dylan."

Melissa was bewildered to hear both love and pride in her sister's voice as she introduced the pair. The man's name sounded familiar. She searched her memory and then asked in surprise, "The same Bryan Healey you dated in high school?"

"The very same," he admitted with an engaging grin.

Taking a closer look at Bryan, Melissa saw a man of about thirty with thick auburn hair. His deep brown eyes assessed her in return and she had the sinking feeling that he knew all about her.

"Hello, Melissa. I'm pleased to meet you." He held out his hand and she took it. His handshake was firm and his voice was definitely friendly, no matter what he was thinking.

The boy with tousled auburn hair, glasses and freckles across his nose wormed his way in front of his dad and held out his hand. "Hi. I'm Dylan. I'm five. Amy is going to marry my daddy and be my mother 'cause my real mom is in heaven. Do you wanna help put our puzzle together?"

Melissa turned her startled gaze to Amy. "What?"

Amy blushed but nodded. "That wasn't exactly how I intended to tell you, but yes, it's true. Bryan and I are engaged."

Melissa fought down a stab of jealousy. She loved her big sister and wanted her to be happy, but this news coming so soon on the heels of her own unhappiness was bittersweet. She gave Amy a quick hug. "Congratulations. Wow, both you and Heather have gotten engaged."

Amy took a deep breath. "And someone else."

Puzzled, Melissa waited for more of an explanation.

Bryan laid a hand on Amy's shoulder. "I think Dylan and I will take off. You and your sister have a lot of catching up to do. Come on, son."

"Aw, do we have to?"

"Yes," he said. "Melissa has been out of the loop for a while and it's going to take some time to get her up to speed."

"What's a loop? Do we got a loop, Dad?"

"Never mind. Go get your jacket." Bryan bent to place a quick kiss on Amy's cheek. "Call me later."

"I will, and thank you."

After he and Dylan left, Melissa sank onto Amy's plush cream-colored damask sofa. "Okay, sis, bring me up to speed."

Amy swept her chin-length blond hair back behind her ears. "The news about the rest of the family can wait. How are you? You sounded so distraught when you called."

"I was, but I'm better now. We can talk about me later. Tell me what the others have been up to."

"My sister, Melissa, doesn't want to talk about herself. That's a first. All right, but I'm not exactly sure where to start."

"Start with Jeremy. How is he? Where is he?"

"He called not long ago. I think I told you he left to go looking for his biological father's family. He has located his grandparents in Florida."

"This is so totally strange. Out of all of us, Jeremy is the most like Dad."

"I know. I was as stunned as everyone else, but truthfully, it hasn't changed the way I feel about him one bit. He's still our brother."

"You're so right, but it makes me wonder what else Mom and Dad haven't told us. You implied that you and Heather weren't the only ones to get engaged. Who else has taken the plunge?"

"The twins started it all."

She stared at her sister in shock. "Heather *and* Chris? No way. To whom?"

"Heather is engaged to Ethan Danes."

"I know you said Ethan on the phone, but do you mean she landed that hunky photographer at the magazine? How did that happen? Heather is so shy, she practically blends into the wallpaper."

"Not anymore. She received an amazing makeover the same day Ellen Manning, the magazine's now ex-makeover expert, took off for greener pastures. You wouldn't believe the change in Heather. She has really come out of her shell. I know it wasn't easy for her, growing up between us."

"Between the homecoming queen and the drama queen, you mean?"

Amy chuckled. "Something like that. Heather isn't as outgoing as you or I, but she has a heart of gold. That's what Ethan fell in love with, not her new look."

"And Chris?"

"That is a slightly longer story. I don't know if you remember the woman reporter the paper hired a few months before you left, Felicity Simmons?"

"Is she the one with long, red hair?"

"That's her. She was working on a story about political corruption when she began receiving threats. At first she blew it off, but it soon became apparent that she had a stalker."

"Let me guess. Brother Chris rides in on a white horse and saves the damsel in distress."

"I think it was his police cruiser, not a horse, but you've got the picture. It turns out that an aide to Mayor

Whitmore had been taking payoffs from a local developer in a land scheme. When Felicity got too close to the truth, he tried to scare her away. When that didn't work, he tried to kidnap her."

"Such wild goings-on in peaceful old Davis Landing. Who would have thought it? Is anyone else in the family getting married?"

"Not at the moment, but Tim is dating Dawn Leroux."

"His administrative assistant?"

"That's right. I think Mom is hearing more wedding bells, but there hasn't been anything official. Enough about our siblings. I want to talk about you."

"There isn't much to talk about. I messed up again, only this time in a *big* way."

"Tell me what happened. You weren't making a lot of sense when you called."

"I know. By the way, thanks for wiring me the money. I don't know what I would have done otherwise. It meant a lot to me. I wasn't sure anyone would want me back after this last stunt."

"Of course we want you here. We're your family. We love you. I told everyone you had called and they were all glad you were okay."

Melissa looked at her sister in sudden panic. "You didn't tell them I was pregnant, did you?"

"Of course not. You asked me not to say anything and I didn't. But you should go see Mom, at least."

"I will. In a day or two."

"Good. Now, tell me about Dean."

Tears stung Melissa's eyes. "I thought he loved me. I wanted...oh, I don't know what I wanted. Maybe to be someone other than Melissa Hamilton.

"At first Dean seemed genuinely happy about the baby. It wasn't until he started talking about how much money my 'old man' would shell out for his grandkid that I started to see Dean for what he was. Someone who wanted me only because I was Wallace Hamilton's daughter. Dean didn't have stars in his eyes when he looked at me, he had dollar signs."

"I'm so sorry. It must have been awful."

"Once I convinced him that my stern, Southern father wasn't going to give his pregnant, runaway daughter a dime, Dean couldn't leave fast enough."

She didn't tell her sister about the way Dean had thrown a wad of money at her and told her to "Get rid of it." She didn't mention how she spent the money paying for another week in the same motel, or about the days and nights she had waited in that dingy place hoping Dean would change his mind and come back for her. Even now, she shuddered to recall the fear and loneliness that kept her pinned in that small room with the snowy TV, peeling, faded purple wallpaper and black mildew climbing the tiles around the chipped bathtub.

After a week, she accepted the fact that he was gone for good. There had been nothing left to do but pack her few belongings and board a bus.

Amy took Melissa's hand and gave it a squeeze. "I'm glad you came home."

Melissa nodded, too choked by emotion to speak.

Amy rose from the sofa. "Why don't I fix us a cup of tea?"

Without waiting for a reply, she moved to the kitchen and Melissa had a few minutes to compose herself. She was so much more emotional of late. One minute she was fine and the next she found herself crying a river. It had to be the pregnancy. She certainly didn't intend to shed one more tear over Dean.

Leaning her head back on the sofa, Melissa closed her eyes. She was so tired. Her nerves had been strung tighter than fiddle strings all day. She needn't have worried. Her big sister was happy to see her in spite of the trouble she brought. Maybe being home wouldn't be so bad after all.

Melissa opened her eyes and wondered where she was. Pushing her hair out of her face, she struggled to sit up. Both her neck and her back protested the change in position. The afghan covering her slid to the floor and she remembered she was at her sister's condo.

The living room was dark except for a single lamp glowing softly on the cherrywood desk in the corner of the room. She squinted at the clock on the wall. It said six-thirty.

The darkness beyond the window had to mean it was six-thirty in the morning. Had she really slept away half the day and all of the night?

Rising, she stretched away her aches, then wiggled her toes and wondered where Amy had stashed her shoes. Looking around, she saw them peeking from under the Monet-styled throw her sister had used to cover her. She folded the blanket, donned her clogs and headed for the kitchen. Now, she was definitely hungry.

A quick survey of the fridge netted her cream cheese and blueberry bagels. She popped the bagels in the toaster, set the kettle on to boil and happily discovered her favorite brand of tea bags in the cupboard beside the sink. She inhaled their pungent fragrance and was instantly struck by memories of herself, her sisters and her mother all enjoying morning tea on the terrace at home.

"You're up early." Amy stood in the kitchen door. Her normally immaculate hair had run amok in the night and the pink terry cloth bathrobe over her pajamas had seen better days.

Melissa felt a stab of guilt. "I hope I didn't wake you."

"No, I have to go into the office early today. How are you feeling?"

"Better, I think. I couldn't believe I was so tired, but I'm as hungry as a horse."

"I'd offer to make breakfast, but I see you've helped yourself. Will you fix me a cup of tea while you're at it?"

"I was just thinking about how we used to join Mom on the terrace for tea in the mornings. Dad would be bellowing from inside the house, 'Nora, where's my briefcase?' Mom would smile and say, 'It's on the hall table. Right where you left it, Wallace.' Then he would come out and give us all a kiss before he left for the office and tell us how pretty we were, but you knew he was really telling Mom how pretty she was."

Amy slipped her arm around Melissa's shoulders. "There will be plenty of good times with Mom and Dad again."

"I hope so."

"Have faith. I don't believe the Lord is ready to take our dad. I think He has other plans for him."

"I wish I shared your belief, but I don't. Not anymore."

"Is that because of Jennifer?"

Jennifer Wilson had been Melissa's best friend since kindergarten. She had been witty and funny—always laughing and often getting them both into trouble. Then, the year Jenny turned sixteen, she died of cancer, and Melissa had been by her side.

Melissa nodded, the ache of grief suddenly sharper than it had been in a long time. "God doesn't care how good someone is or how hard you pray. Dead is dead."

"Oh, honey. You are so wrong about that. We can't know what God has planned for any of us, but He loves us. And dead isn't dead. Death is simply crossing over to a better place where we get to meet Jesus face-to-face."

Melissa used the whistling kettle as an excuse to end the conversation. "Looks like the water is ready. Do you want cream or sugar in your tea?"

Amy hesitated, but seemed to understand that Melissa wanted to change the subject. "A little cream."

The conversation lagged until the women were seated at the table. Melissa finished half her bagel before Amy spoke again.

"What are your plans, Melissa?"

"I plan to finish the rest of my breakfast."

"I'm serious."

"The funny part is, so am I. I can't think beyond the next fifteen minutes, let alone make plans for my future."

"You have someone else's future to think about."

"Don't you think I know that? I'm not mother material. I mean, look at me! I can't take care of myself. I'm a college dropout. I've always lived at home. I've never had to take care of anyone. I don't even have a job." Melissa's bagel suddenly lost its appeal. She laid it on her plate, then picked up her spoon and stirred the contents of her cup.

"You have a job."

She glanced at Amy and raised one eyebrow. "I do?"

"Dad wouldn't let Tim fill your position at the paper. Instead, he placed you on indefinite leave. You still have a job—one with benefits, like health insurance, which will come in very handy."

"Do you see what I mean? I never even thought about insurance."

Amy reached across the table and laid a hand on Melissa's arm. "Don't be so hard on yourself. You've had a lot on your mind. I know this can't be easy for you."

"I wish none of this had happened. I wish Dad wasn't sick and I wish I'd never met Dean, or run off with him. I wish I could erase the past six months and go back to being a bored copy aide at the *Dispatch,* answering phones and compiling paperwork for the editors."

"Oh, Melissa."

"It's not possible. I know, but I wish it were."

"It's going to be hard, but you have to start looking ahead."

Melissa remembered Richard's advice and nodded. "I need to take things one small step at a time."

"That's right." Amy smiled and took a sip of her tea.

"I guess if I have a job, that's a start."

"That's a good start, although a few things have changed at Hamilton Media that you should know about."

"Like what? Besides Tim's running the show now that Jeremy has left. You mentioned Ellen Manning was now the magazine's *ex*-makeover expert. I never really liked her anyway. Don't tell me the Gordons have retired?"

"I doubt you or I will live to see that day. No, Jeremy had to fire our accountant, Curtis Resnick."

"You're kidding. They've been friends for ages."

"Curtis was embezzling from us. Because they had been such good friends, Jeremy fired him instead of turning him in to the police. That was really what sparked the dustup between Dad and Jeremy."

"I see. Poor Jeremy. And poor Tim, to have to take over when things were in such an uproar. How is he handling things?"

"He was pretty tough on the staff, at first. They started calling him Typhoon Tim behind his back, but I have to admit he has found his stride. The business is doing well with him at the helm."

"Anything else I need to know?"

Amy looked down at her teacup. "Not right at the moment."

Melissa had the feeling there was more, but she didn't want to pressure her sister.

Suddenly, Amy looked up and said, "Why don't you move back home with Mom? The place is certainly big enough."

The idea was tempting, but somehow Melissa knew that if she did, things were never going to change. She would let her well-meaning family take over more and more of her responsibilities instead of facing them herself. "I think I'd rather get a place of my own."

"You're welcome to stay here until you find something. I only have one bedroom, but you're welcome to the sofa."

"Thanks. I may have to stay for a little while."

"Melissa, you haven't said what you intend to do about the baby."

"You noticed that?"

"Yes, I did."

"I've been thinking about what I should do for months. I know I told you the baby belonged with me, but in my heart, I also know I'm not cut out to be a mother."

"Have you thought about adoption?"

"I've thought about it a lot."

"And?"

"I'm not sure. I mean—I may be the pits as a mother, but what if some weirdo gets her or him? You hear horror stories all the time."

"There is someone at the paper you should talk to. She adopted a child not long ago. I think she might be able to put your mind at ease on that score. But there is something else you need to think about. Dean may be out of the picture as far as you're concerned, but he has exactly the same rights to your baby as you do."

"The guy is a jerk."

"Granted, but jerk or not, he's the baby's father. He may have to surrender his rights the same way you will in order to place the child for adoption. Before you make any decisions you need to know where you stand legally. You need to talk to Richard McNeil."

"Mr. McNeil can see you now, Miss Hamilton."

"Thank you, Mrs. Woodrow." Melissa rose from her chair in the reception area and followed Richard's secretary down a mahogany-paneled hall to his office. Richard stood holding the door open and waiting for her.

"Hello again, Melissa. Come on in." He indicated one of a pair of burgundy leather chairs that faced his desk. He was wearing another beautifully tailored suit, a dark blue pinstripe with a light blue dress shirt. This time a patterned tie completed the look. The outfit made his eyes seem darker, more intense. Perhaps it was only her imagination.

"I'm thankful you could see me on such short notice." Melissa took a seat and plucked at the front of her wine-colored velvet tunic. It was another loose-fitting top that she hoped would hide her expanding waistline. She kept her handbag in her lap.

"You said it was important." Instead of sitting behind the desk, he sat in the chair next to hers.

Melissa's grip tightened on her handbag until her knuckles whitened. This would be the best thing for her child, but how did she go about telling someone who had known her all her life that she didn't want her own baby? What would he think?

He leaned forward in the chair and laid a comforting hand over her tightly clenched ones. "Anything you say to me will be kept in the strictest confidence."

She managed a weak smile. "I know that. After all, you never told anyone I was the culprit behind the Reindeer heists."

He chuckled and sat back. "No. I never squealed on you. Although how you managed to steal nine of them in one night without getting caught remains a mystery to this day. You weren't old enough to drive."

"I borrowed some shopping carts from the Piggy Wiggly parking lot."

"Ah! And how did you get the deer into the school and dressed in the basketball team's jerseys?"

"They looked good, didn't they? The Davis Landing Bucks weren't winning any games that year. I thought we needed a whole new team. Getting into the building was a bit difficult. Getting them dressed wasn't hard."

"I always figured it was an inside job."

"Remember the night watchman, Mr. Chapman?"

"Don't tell me that he helped you, after all? I thought the reason you came to me was so that he wouldn't lose his job."

"He didn't exactly help, but he did step out often for a smoke break. He'd leave the gym door propped open sometimes. Once we—I was inside, it was easy to wait until he left to make his rounds again. It didn't seem fair of the school board to let him go because of my prank."

"You did the right thing when you called me and confessed that you and Jennifer had stolen Rudolph and his team from the Christmas display in front of the Wilcox home."

She tipped her head to the side. "I never told you Jennifer was the one who helped me."

"You two were thick as thieves back then. Who else would have helped you pull off a stunt like that?"

"She always had the coolest ideas."

"And you were the one who couldn't let someone else take the blame. So what is this about, Melissa? Not more stolen reindeer, I hope?"

She looked down at her hands, not wanting to see the expression on his face. "I wish that was all. I came today because I need your help."

"I'm listening."

There was no way to beat around this bush. She gave up trying and blurted out, "I'm pregnant."

Chapter Three

A long silence met Melissa's declaration. She chanced a peek at Richard. She expected him to be stunned, but she was surprised to see that he looked…hurt and disappointed. The expression was fleeting. When he met her gaze, he smiled and said, "What kind of help can I give you?"

So far, so good. "I want to find out about adoption."

"You want to place your baby for adoption?" He looked astounded.

She stared down at her handbag and began to open and close the clasp without noticing what she was doing. "I think it would be the best thing, don't you?"

Click, click.

"Just because I've made a mess of my life is no reason to mess up my kid's life. Right?"

Click, click.

"I mean, look at me. I've only got a job because my daddy owns the paper. I'm a college dropout. I don't even have a place to live. I'm staying with Amy, but she only has one bedroom and her sofa isn't that great to sleep on."

She continued clicking her bag open and shut until Richard placed his large, warm hand over hers and held them still. "Melissa, are you sure about this?"

His touch was so gentle and comforting. She looked into his bright blue eyes filled with kindness and it was as if a dam broke inside her. Her words came out in a rush of emotion. "I'm not sure of anything. I have no idea what I should do. My father is always sure about everything. My mother is the same way. My brothers and my sisters, they all seem to know what they want in life. Even you! You knew you wanted to be a lawyer and that was that.

"What's wrong with me that I can't see my way? Why is my life such a fog when everyone around me sees things so clearly? Why am I so different? My family puts up with me because they love me, but I always disappoint them. I'm tired of forever making the wrong choices. I want to start making the right decisions. How do you do it?"

"I can't answer that for you, Melissa. All I can say is that life isn't about making one choice and then everything falls into place. I face tough choices all the time. I use my faith as a guide and I try to make the choices I believe God wants me to make. Sometimes I fail."

"Then what do you do?"

"I try to take an honest look at why I made that decision. Then I try to fix what went wrong."

"That's what I want to do. I want to fix what I did wrong."

"Have you discussed this with your parents?"

She raised her chin. "No. This has to be my decision."

"That's true, but this isn't an easy task. It will require a strong commitment and you will need your family's support. Have you been to see your father?"

"My sister, Amy, is helping me. I haven't told anyone else. I'm certainly not ready to have Dad read me the riot act."

"I think you're misjudging him."

"No, if there's one thing I do know, it's that Dad is going to be furious when he hears this. Oh, he won't be surprised. He always said I'd come to no good if I didn't mend my ways. I think that's what I hate most about this. I ended up proving him right."

"Nothing has to be decided today, Melissa. Here is what I want you to do. Sleep on this decision. If tomorrow you still feel this is what you want, call me and I'll help find a suitable couple for the child."

"But tomorrow is Saturday."

"I have special hours for special clients. Call me. I'll be here."

"Amy mentioned that Dean has a right to the baby and that he could block the adoption."

"That's true. As the child's father, he can."

"Do we have to tell him about it? He told me to get rid of the baby. He doesn't want anything to do with us."

"Many people say things in the heat of the moment that they later regret. Either way, legally, we will need his consent. Do you know how to contact him?"

"I'll give you the name of his band manager. He should be able to find Dean."

"Good." Richard stood and helped Melissa to her feet. Slipping his arm around her shoulder, he gave her a quick hug. "I'm not an adoption attorney, I do corporate law, but I have a good friend who runs an adoption clinic. With his help, I'll take care of all the legal paperwork. Try not to worry. Everything will work out."

"That's easy for you to say. You aren't the one who's going to look like a hippo in three months."

Chuckling, he placed a finger under her chin and tilted her face up. "Courage, Melissa."

She took a deep breath. "If you insist, I'll give it a try."

After Melissa left his office, Richard sat in the black swivel chair behind his desk. Poor kid, she'd really done it this time. He, like most people, had considered her capricious and careless. To hear in her own words how lost and alone she felt pulled at his heartstrings.

She needed someone she could talk to. One of her own family members made the most sense, but he suspected the Hamilton family had just about all they could deal with at the moment. An idea began to form in the back of his mind.

He leaned forward and pressed the intercom. "Margaret, please get my sister on the phone. She should still be at her office at the university."

"Yes, sir."

He leaned back and waited. Melissa needed a place to stay and he had an extra bedroom at his home. If Angela and Dave didn't have any objections, maybe Melissa could stay with them.

Before he got too far into his plan, Margaret buzzed him to let him know his sister was on the phone. He picked up line one. "Hi, Angela. I'm sorry to interrupt you at work. Are you busy? This could wait."

"I'm swamped, but now is as good a time as any. I was getting ready to call and let you know I'm going to be late again tonight. Do you think the girls will mind pizza?"

"They'll survive. Do you know what Dave has planned?"

"He said this morning that he would be working late at the house. He's getting the rest of the electrical lines run tonight so the drywallers can start putting up Sheetrock tomorrow. What did you need?"

"Do you remember Melissa Hamilton?"

"Certainly. I had her in my English 101 class last year. She was a bright student, but she never seemed to have much focus. Once she turned in the most amazing paper on women writers from the South, but her next piece was terrible. It was as if she didn't want to succeed. Why do you ask about her?"

"She's in a bit of trouble and she's looking for a place to live. If you didn't mind, I thought I'd offer to let her stay with us while you and Dave are there."

"It's your home, of course, but why can't she stay with her mother? The Hamilton house is bigger than yours."

"I'm not at liberty to discuss it, but she has her reasons. I only thought of it because you mentioned hiring someone to help with the kids until your workload lets up. I know that Dave is spending all his free time getting your house repaired. With Melissa living at our place, it might make things easier for you. It's just an idea."

"I did like her, and I certainly don't mind helping someone out. I've received more than my fair share of help from friends and family since the fire. It would feel good to give back a little. You're right, it might make things easier. I'll talk it over with Dave and give you an answer in the morning."

"Great. Thanks, sis."

Richard hung up the phone. His sense of satisfaction was quickly followed by a niggling doubt. Was he helping or hurting Melissa by trying to make things easier for her?

* * *

Melissa let herself into Amy's apartment. Tossing her handbag on the desk, she kicked off her shoes and dropped onto the sofa. Lassitude crept over her and she longed for a nap. A nap at one o'clock in the afternoon? Did being pregnant make everyone exhausted by the middle of the day? How had her mother managed to do this five times? Once with twins, no less!

A single glance at her puffy ankles was enough to convince Melissa she needed to put her feet up. It didn't take much extra effort to pull the coverlet over her shoulders and settle her head on one of Amy's bright green throw pillows. The next time she opened her eyes, the clock on the wall said two-thirty and she was starving. Again.

A handful of carrot and celery sticks pilfered from her sister's refrigerator took the edge off her hunger pangs, but she wanted something more, something substantial. As she surveyed the contents of her sister's cupboards, fridge and freezer, Melissa settled on a plan of action. Lasagna, garlic toast and a fresh salad would make a wonderful dinner. Never one to do much cooking, Melissa searched for and found a cookbook with full color photos of the finished product.

Her mother was fond of saying, "If you can read, you can cook." Usually she had been talking to the boys at Sunday dinner when they started complaining about their bachelor existences and living off takeout. Well, there was no time like the present to test her mother's theory. Wouldn't Amy be surprised when she came home?

Setting to work with a sudden burst of energy,

Melissa diced, chopped and simmered away the rest of the afternoon. By five-thirty the apartment was filled with the smells of tomato sauce, oregano, basil and baking bread. She was setting the table when she heard Amy's key in the door.

Amy walked in and stopped short. "I must be in the wrong apartment. Something smells wonderful."

"Surprise! I thought I would make dinner to say thanks for putting me up—and for putting up with me."

"Melissa, I didn't even know you could cook."

"You'd better reserve judgment until after you taste it. The bread is sort of burned on the bottom and the tomato sauce didn't thicken the way the recipe said it would."

"I'm still impressed. Let me change and call Bryan first."

Melissa's pride in her accomplishment plummeted. "You have plans for tonight, don't you? Of course you do. It's Friday."

"Bryan had asked me out, but he'll understand."

Melissa plopped into one of the padded Windsor chairs that surrounded Amy's table. "No, don't change your plans for me."

"I don't want all your hard work to go to waste. Bryan and I can change our date to Saturday."

"Really?"

"Sure."

"No, don't do that." Dejected, she straightened the silverware beside one plate.

Amy came across the room and sat beside her. "Do you think you made enough to feed two more people?"

Melissa brightened, "I'll have to throw together a little more salad, but sure."

"Great. I'll ask Bryan and Dylan to come over, then we can still catch a movie afterward."

Mollified, but still unhappy that she hadn't thought about asking her sister if she had plans, Melissa retreated to the kitchen while her sister went to change. Stacks of tomato-stained pans and bowls met her gaze. When had she made such a mess? Even the stovetop was splattered with burned sauce. She hurried to load the dishwasher and wipe up before her sister noticed the disaster in her normally immaculate kitchen.

Later, with Amy and Bryan heaping praise on her for the meal, Melissa began to feel that she hadn't completely blown the couple's evening. Dylan cleaned his plate in short order.

"You'd better hurry, Dad. We don't want to miss the movie."

Bryan smiled and rubbed his son's unruly hair. "Take it easy, tiger. We won't miss a thing. I'm sorry we have to eat and run, Melissa."

She waved aside his concerns. "The next time I decide to whip up a feast, I'll make sure no one has plans."

Amy sent Bryan on to the car with Dylan, then she turned to Melissa and said, "I know you've been worried about how you were going to tell everyone about your pregnancy. I sort of took matters into my own hands."

"What do you mean?"

"I've called everyone except Dad. I'll let you tell him in your own time."

Melissa's hands clenched into fists at her side. She struggled to hide her sense of betrayal. "Amy, I wish you hadn't done that."

"I understand that you wanted to tell the others

yourself, but this way you don't have to face everyone and rehash the story over and over. Now, it's done and you won't have to worry about it any longer."

Her anger at her sister faded quickly. Amy was right. It *was* a relief knowing that everyone had been told. Melissa gave Amy a wry smile. "My big sister is still trying to find ways to make life easy for me."

"Just this one last time. Then I'm done, honest."

Melissa bit her bottom lip, then asked, "What did they say?"

"I'll spare you the brotherly comments. Once everyone digested the news, they were willing to support you in any way they can."

"And Mom?"

"Mom said she would call you."

"That was it?"

"That was it." Amy started for the door, but turned back, a look of indecision on her face. "Melissa, before you talk to Mom, there is one more thing I think you need to know."

"What?"

"It's about Dad. There's a rumor being spread around that he had an affair and that it resulted in a love child."

"What? I don't believe it. Who would say such a thing?"

"I don't believe it, either. The story came out in the *Observer*'s gossip column. It hinted that the woman was someone well-known in the community. As you can imagine, all of this has been hard on Mom."

"I guess so. Poor Mom."

After her sister left to catch the latest action-adventure flick, Melissa sank onto the sofa. The sudden quiet pressed in, making her feel lonely and tired. Tired but not sleepy. She tried watching TV but nothing on the ninety-three cable channels held her attention. Giving up after flipping through them twice, she shut the set off and silence ruled.

What would she say to her mother when she called? As much as she disliked Amy's interference, Melissa had to admit she was glad the news was out to the family. It would make the next meeting with her siblings easier, if not the next meeting with her parents.

The harsh ring of the phone suddenly ripped into the quiet and Melissa jumped. Another shrill ring sent her scooting off the sofa to look at Amy's caller ID— although she suspected who it was before she saw the number displayed. Of course it couldn't be some tele-marketer selling time-shares. No, it was her mom.

Melissa's fingers trembled slightly as she picked up the receiver. "Hello."

"Oh, Melissa, it's so good to hear your voice."

The love and concern pouring through those few words was all it took to crumple Melissa's defenses. She sank to the floor and began to weep. "I'm so sorry, Mom," she managed to get out between sobs.

"Don't cry, honey. Please, you're breaking my heart."

"I don't know why I do these things. I know they'll hurt you, but I can't seem to stop myself. I know you're worried about Daddy, and I didn't want to burden you with this, but I didn't know where else to go."

"It's all right. You did the right thing. With God's help, we'll deal with this, too."

"Don't tell Daddy. Please don't tell him," Melissa begged.

"Honey, he's going to find out sooner or later."

"I know. I'll tell him—but just not yet."

"This is so difficult over the phone. Why don't you come home, sweetheart?"

"Because I got myself into the mess and I'm going to deal with it without adding to your troubles, Mom. If I come home you'll try and fix it like you always do. This I have to take care of by myself."

"I respect that, Melissa, I do, but I think you should reconsider."

"Tell me about Daddy. How is he, really?"

The pause on the other end of the line let Melissa know her mother wasn't ready to change the subject. After a deep sigh, Nora said, "I think you would be shocked to see the way this has aged him, but his spirit is still as strong as ever. Sometimes, I think he is in complete denial. It's been hard on everyone to see him laid low, but you know your father. When someone says he can't do something, he had to prove them wrong. Honestly, I think his stubborn streak works better than any of the drugs they give him."

"When you see him, will you tell him that I love him. Tell him that I'm sorry I'm such a disappointment."

"You aren't a disappointment, honey."

"Right, and Elvis isn't dead. He lives over on Main Street in Hickory Mills."

"If your father wasn't expecting me at the hospital, I'd come over to Amy's now. I can call him and tell him I've changed my plans."

Sorry for her flippant attitude, Melissa said, "No, don't do that."

"If you won't come home, at least meet me some-where where we can talk."

"I'm not sure."

"Please, Melissa."

"All right. I can do that."

"Why don't we meet for lunch tomorrow at Betty's Bakeshoppe? We can have tea and catch up on things, and cry on each other's shoulders. I've been where you are, honey. I understand what you're going through."

"Betty's will be fine."

"Good. Tomorrow at two?"

"I'll be there."

"You won't run off again, will you, Melissa? I'm so worried about you."

"No, Mom. I'm back in town to stay." As Melissa made the promise she wondered if she was brave enough to keep it.

After talking to her mother, Melissa lay down on the sofa and curled onto her side. A deep sadness settled in her heart. She had caused everyone so much pain. Her hand moved to the swell of her stomach. She poked the bulge softly with one finger. "You do realize that you're the cause of this. Besides breaking my mother's heart, you've made it hard to button my jeans."

A strange, tiny flutter deep inside Melissa caught her by surprise. She pressed her hand tightly against the feeling.

There it was again!

A sense of wonder replaced the sadness she had been feeling. "You moved! I think you kicked me!"

Melissa sat up and waited to see if she had imagined it. No, it was definitely a thump. Oh, why wasn't Amy home? Melissa wanted to share this moment with someone. Richard's face flashed into her mind. He would understand what a thrill this was. Would Dean feel the same way if she gave him the chance? She cupped both hands around her tummy.

"Are you knocking? Do you want out? Don't be in a hurry to get here, kid. Life isn't all that grand. Your daddy's run off. Your mother is a fool—and these could be the lyrics to a country-western song."

A bubble of giddiness rose in Melissa and erupted into a laugh. "I can't believe I'm talking to my stomach."

Another faint thump, thump left no doubt. Her baby had moved. The thought was closely followed by the knowledge that he, or she, would soon be someone else's baby.

Melissa's merriment faded. Conflicting emotions tumbled through her heart. Longing and misery, amazement and sorrow. She would give her child away as soon as it arrived in the world.

"I hope you know this is the best thing for both of us. I'm not the kind of person who would make a good mother. Someday maybe you'll understand that," she whispered. "Maybe someday you'll forgive me."

Melissa tipped her head back and sighed. One more giant heartache loomed on her horizon. Where would she find the strength she needed to do the right thing?

Chapter Four

It was almost ten o'clock the next morning before Melissa worked up the nerve to call Richard McNeil. The level of candy in the clear glass bowl Amy always kept on hand had dropped significantly and a pile of discarded foil wrappers littered the desktop.

Thinking about putting her baby up for adoption was one thing. Actually making the call to tell Richard to start the process was a whole different story. Her mind said this was the right thing to do, but her heart seemed bent on arguing.

"One small step at a time, girl," she murmured as she grasped the receiver and held it to her ear. With her free hand, she punched in the numbers she had memorized, then she wadded the silver wrappers into a ball and tossed them into the trash can.

When she told Richard about her decision, would he think she was throwing her baby away?

His secretary answered on the second ring and put Melissa through to him.

"Richard McNeil speaking." His voice came across sounding curt and professional. Her courage wavered.

"Richard, this is Melissa Hamilton."

"Melissa, how are you today?"

"Honestly? I'm frightened, confused, nervous and about to expire from an overdose of chocolate kisses," she said in a rush. "How are you?"

"I'm fine. Would it make you feel better to know that is how most people feel when they have to call an attorney?"

She heard his amusement and she relaxed a little. "At least I'm not calling from jail."

"Always a good sign in my books."

"I wanted to let you know that I've made up my mind."

"And?"

"I want you to help me find this child a good home." She winced inwardly at her choice of words. This wasn't like finding someone to take in a stray puppy.

"Melissa, are you sure about this?"

"Yes. Tell me what I need to do." If only she could feel as sure as she sounded.

"I'll get the paperwork started. Have you thought about what type of adoption you want?"

"What do you mean?"

"Do you want an open adoption, where you choose and meet the adoptive parents and remain in limited contact with the child? Or would you rather not know anything about the family?"

"Open sounds better, doesn't it?"

"That's up to you."

"I guess I'll have to think about that. What else do I need to know?"

"As I told you, I have a friend who is an adoption attorney. I'll have him put together some information for you and then we can go over it after you've had a chance to read it and think about it. After that, we'll form an adoption plan. If you want to meet the prospective parents, I'll set up some interviews."

"That sounds good." With Richard to help her, maybe this wasn't going to be so bad after all.

"I'll draft a letter to Dean to let him know what you're planning. He won't be able to relinquish his rights until after the baby is born. You understand that you can't, either. Nothing will be final until the baby arrives."

"I understand that."

"Good. There is something else I'd like to discuss. You mentioned that you don't want to move back home. Do you still feel that way?"

"Absolutely. I've talked to my mother and she understands how I feel."

"In that case, I have an offer for you to consider. My sister and her family recently had a fire at their home. While their house is being renovated, they're staying with me. To make a long story short, Angela is working a lot of overtime and Dave is spending his free time trying to get their house repaired. That leaves the girls with me or on their own. My sister has been thinking about hiring someone to help with the housework and entertain the girls when she can't get home. Would you be interested in the job? She can't pay much, but you would get free room and board. You would have a bedroom and a bath to yourself. Are you interested?"

"You're offering me a job?"

"Let's call it a temporary solution to several

problems. My sister needs help and you need a place to stay. It won't be for more than five or six weeks, but that should give you time to find a place of your own."

"That's very kind of you, Richard."

"This isn't kindness. It's a business offer. Unless, of course, you really like sleeping on Amy's couch. In that case, I'm sure Angela can find someone else to help."

Melissa gave the cream-colored divan a sour glance. It was pretty, but as a bed, it didn't quite make the grade. "If you're sure this is a job and not charity, I accept your offer. When do I start?"

"I could help you move in tomorrow. Would that be too soon?"

"Not at all. Tomorrow will be fine."

"Good. I think you'll like the girls. Samantha is twelve and Lauren is eight. They're old enough that they don't need a lot of supervision, but they're still too young to leave alone for any length of time."

Something in his voice made her question him further. "I get the feeling there is something you aren't telling me."

"The girls have had some trouble adjusting since the fire, especially Samantha. Usually she is as happy as a lark, but since the fire, she has been unhappy and withdrawn. I'm hoping that having someone new in the house will help take her mind off of things."

"I'm sure we'll get along. I come from a big family, remember?"

"I remember. I'll pick you up tomorrow afternoon. What time works for you?"

"I think I can have my duffel bag packed by four."

"So, I won't need to rent a moving van?"

"No, not this time."

"Great. My back was aching at the thought."

"I'll see you tomorrow." She chuckled as she hung up the phone. In spite of her current situation, Richard always seemed to make her smile. But then, he always had been able to make her laugh.

Melissa pulled open the glass door to Betty's Bakeshoppe a few minutes before two that afternoon and was instantly surrounded by the mouthwatering smells of cinnamon rolls, aromatic coffee and baked apples. The shop was more than a coffee house. Over the past twenty years Betty and her daughters had expanded the bakery into a restaurant area and had added a small used bookstore at one end. Betty's Bakeshoppe now took up three connecting shops along the downtown street. But it was Betty's excellent cooking and the convenient location across from the Hamilton Media building that made it a prime meeting place for employees and downtown business people.

Looking around, Melissa saw several faces she recognized from the paper. The Saturday-afternoon lunch crowd was long gone, but there were still a few customers lingering over their desserts. She spied her mother seated at a table by the window in the corner, where shelves made a partial wall between the eatery and the bookstore.

A petite woman, Nora Hamilton might have been mistaken for one of her own children if not for the strands of silver in her shoulder-length blond hair. She was dressed simply in a belted red dress with a wide white collar and white trim on the short sleeves.

Nora's face brightened when she caught sight of her daughter, but not before Melissa noticed how tired her mother looked. Guilt gnawed at Melissa's conscience. She was responsible for adding to her mother's already heavy worries.

Threading her way between the tables, Melissa watched her mother rise. An instant later she found herself gathered in a warm embrace, one she returned fiercely as a tear slipped from the corner of her eye. She had missed her family more than she realized.

Nora was the first to draw back. "I'm so glad you came. Let me look at you."

"Mom, I'm fine." Melissa wiped the tear from her cheek with the back of her hand and submitted to her mother's scrutiny.

"I believe it now that I see you with my own eyes. You had us all worried."

They took their seats and Melissa glanced around the room to avoid looking at her mother. Embarrassment made the sudden silence painful. Instead of talking about herself, she sought a neutral subject. "I've always liked coming to the Bakeshoppe."

"I remember how you would beg your father to meet us here for lunch when you were little."

"I thought it was the coolest place. I'd never been to any other store where the drapes were painted on the windows. I see they still have that rug painted on the old wood floor in front of the cash register."

"Remember how you used to stand on it and hop on and off? You told me you could make it fly."

"Mom, I think I must have been four then."

Nora smiled softly as she looked back in time. "It

always made your father chuckle. Time goes by too fast."

"Then I grew up and made Dad mad all the time."

"Not all the time, dear."

"More times than not."

"You went through a very difficult time after Jennifer died. We knew that but we couldn't seem to help you."

Talking about Jennifer was the last thing Melissa wanted to do. Fortunately, Justine, Betty's daughter, came up to the table with her order pad in hand. "Mrs. Hamilton, it's nice to see you. How is Mr. Hamilton? We've been keeping him in our prayers."

"He's doing better, Justine. Thank you for asking." Nora glanced toward the kitchen. "Is your mother here?"

"No, she had to leave early today. Melissa, I haven't seen you in a while."

"I've been out of town, but I'm back now."

"What can I get for you ladies? Our special today is apple pie."

After ordering a slice of pie and a cup of tea, Melissa waited until Justine served them and then moved away. Before she could decide how to bring up the subject that hung in the air between them like an elephant in the middle of the room, her mother reached across the table and laid a hand on Melissa's arm.

"I want you to know that I understand what you're feeling, Melissa. I faced the same thing when I was pregnant with Jeremy."

"I couldn't believe it when Amy told me Jeremy wasn't Dad's son. How? I mean, who was his father?"

"His name was Paul Anderson and we were engaged to be married. We were young and careless. We were in love, and we thought nothing else mattered. Then he died in a motorcycle accident. I didn't even know I was pregnant. A few months later, I met your father."

"Did he know?"

"Not at first. It took a lot of courage to tell him, but I knew it was the right thing to do."

Melissa wanted to ask her mother another question, but she wasn't sure she wanted to hear the answer. She picked up her spoon and began to stir her tea, but couldn't contain her troubling thoughts. "Was that the only reason you married Daddy? For the sake of the baby?"

"Melissa, look at me," Nora said softly.

Melissa raised her eyes and met her mother's unflinching gaze.

"I fell deeply in love with your father, and I have thanked God every day of my life that He sent Wallace to me. Never doubt that."

Melissa had always believed her parents loved each other. It was good to know that that part of her life hadn't been a sham. She looked down at her teacup again. "Did you ever think about giving Jeremy up for adoption?"

"Of course I thought about it. I prayed about it, and I wavered back and forth, but in the end I knew it wasn't what God wanted for me. Are you thinking about adoption?"

"Yes. I've already spoken to Richard McNeil. He is going to help me find a family. In a way, it's a relief to have finally made a decision." Melissa forked a bite of sweet, tart apples and featherlight crust into her mouth.

Nora's eyes filled with sadness. "I can't tell you what to do, sweetheart, but please give this a lot of thought and prayer. God has a plan for all of us, even if we can't see it. It would be hard to raise a child alone, but I would help all I could. I know your father will feel the same way. This is, after all, our first grandchild."

It was hard for Melissa to swallow her food past the lump that pushed up in her throat. "I'm sorry, but I'm not like you. I don't have what it takes to be a mother. I don't have patience or good sense. This child will be better off with someone who wants a kid. Besides, I'm not so sure that Daddy will want anything to do with this baby."

"You're judging him harshly, Melissa. It will be a shock for him, but he'll come around. You'll see."

"You always believe the best of people."

"And I'm rarely disappointed. What about the baby's father? Will he help?"

Melissa pushed her pie aside. "He doesn't want either of us. We didn't fit into his big plans."

"I wish I could ease your heartache, Melissa. Things look bleak now, but God heals all wounds. Have faith, honey, and give it some time."

"I wish I shared your beliefs, but I don't. See, that's one more reason this baby belongs somewhere else."

"Giving your child up for adoption takes great courage and great love. Whatever you decide, your family will support you."

Melissa struggled with the next question on her mind. "Amy told me there is a rumor going around about Dad and another woman. Do you think it's true?"

"I know your father, and I know he has been a faithful husband to me since the day we wed. I will admit he's not always an easy man to live with, but his love for me has never wavered. Never.

"Our family has been blessed with material wealth

and much more. There are people who don't have what we have and resent that fact. Any influential family can find itself the target of jealously and rumors."

"I guess you're right, Mom."

"I am. Now, enough about our tale of woes. Tell me what it was like traveling around the country with a rock band."

"You do *not* want to know that stuff."

Nora sighed. "I imagine you're right. You might not believe this, but I did envy you your freedom to pick up and go. I've always wanted to travel, to see the world and exotic places."

"Why don't you?"

"Your father has always been too busy with the company for us to spend more than a week away. Perhaps we'll travel someday. When he's better."

Behind the bookshelves, former Hamilton Media employee Curtis Resnick replaced the novel he had been feigning interest in and left quietly by the book room door. He could barely contain his glee. Once again, the Hamiltons had provided the perfect fodder for the town's gossip mill. Now, all he had to do was deliver this delightful nugget to Ellen Manning. Her new position at the *Observer* made her the perfect accomplice for his little plan.

The Hamilton family would continue to pay for ousting him and damaging his reputation, not to mention his finances by making him repay the money he had "borrowed." The town was already abuzz with speculation about Wallace's affair and the fact that Nora Hamilton had been pregnant with another man's child when they wed. The Hamiltons might pretend they were better than all the rest of Davis Landing, but he would take them down a peg or two. No, a peg or two wouldn't be enough. He wanted to destroy them and all they stood for.

Curtis smiled as he thought about the youngest daughter following in her mother's footsteps. She couldn't have played into his hands better if she had tried. He would have to do a little digging, maybe even a little stalking, but he was sure he could come up with some photos to go along with the story. Soon everyone in town would know about Melissa Hamilton's illegitimate child.

Chapter Five

Sitting on the front seat beside Richard in his car, Melissa waited eagerly for a glimpse of his house as he turned first left, then right, down the quiet streets in one of the newer residential areas of Davis Landing. She had never been to his home, and she found herself wondering what kind of house he would have chosen for himself. The dwellings they passed were large with spacious lawns, but they lacked the mature oak and pine trees that graced the homes in her old neighborhood. When he turned, at last, into a circular drive, she was pleased to see a modern, Colonial-style house.

The two-story wood and stone home had wide multipaned windows spaced evenly on either side of an oval porch that jutted out in front. The two tall white columns that supported the porch gave the home a regal appearance. Yew trees in matching white containers were set as accents beside the front door. Yellow climbing roses covered a wrought-iron trellis at the side of the garage. The low box hedge bordering the property gave it a neat, well-cared-for and stately air. Beyond the house, the backyard rose at a gentle slope to a densely wooded hillside.

Richard parked in the drive out front and after getting her bag from the trunk, he held her door open. Melissa got out and saw Angela Hart coming down the walk. Melissa remembered his sister fondly from college. Angela's happy personality, vibrant green eyes and beautiful, thick red hair worn in a braid down her back had always made Melissa think of Ireland. At her side was a tall burly man with brown hair, a neat goatee and a wide smile.

"Welcome to our temporary home," Angela said as she extended her hand.

"Thank you, Mrs. Hart."

Angela gave Melissa's hand a quick squeeze. "Don't thank me until after you meet our hooligans, and please call me Angela. This is my husband, Dave."

"How do you do?" Melissa said.

"We can't thank you enough for agreeing to help look after the girls. It surely does take a load off my mind." Melissa's hand was engulfed in his as he gave it a hearty shake.

"I'm happy I can help."

Angela said, "Come in and meet the rest of our family. Your room is ready. I hope you like it."

"I'm sure I will." Melissa followed Richard's sister and brother-in-law into the house. The oversize white front door opened into a spacious foyer tiled in pale native stone. Beyond was a formal living room decorated in tastefully muted shades of browns and beiges with rich, textured fabrics covering a large sofa and matching chairs. The oak floors gleamed with warmth as the tall windows framed in pale gold drapes let the autumn sunshine pour in.

Melissa glanced at Richard and found him watching her closely. She smiled. The house fit him exactly. It was masculine, yet not overpowering or dark.

Giggles and the patter of feet on the stairs announced the arrival of one of Richard's nieces. The girl rushed to her mother's side, looking Melissa over with frank curiosity. She wore a pair of faded jeans and a yellow T-shirt with a rock band logo on it.

Angela slipped her arms across the child's shoulders. "This is Lauren. Lauren, this is Miss Hamilton. She is the lady who is going to be staying with us for a while."

Lauren obviously took after her mother in looks. Her curly, bright red hair was cut short and framed a round face dotted with a liberal sprinkling of freckles. Her green eyes studied Melissa intently. She gave a bob of a curtsy. "Pleased to meet you, Miss Hamilton."

"Please call me Melissa. Miss Hamilton sounds so formal."

"Where is Samantha?" Dave asked.

Lauren said, "She's upstairs."

"Please go tell her our guest is here," Angela said.

"She knows. She says she doesn't need a babysitter."

Angela gave Melissa an apologetic look. Dave patted his wife's arm. "I'll go talk to her."

"I'm coming." A sullen voice from the stairs caused Melissa to glance up.

Samantha Hart had inherited her father's straight, dark hair and brown eyes. She was dressed in jeans and a red T-shirt and she sauntered down the steps with evident reluctance. She sent a covert glance toward

Melissa. On one hand, it was apparent that the girl was trying to look bored, but it was equally obvious that she was curious about the woman who would be living with them. She stopped beside her mother and crossed her arms over her chest.

"Pleased to meet you, Miss Hamilton," she drawled, but Melissa could tell she wasn't pleased in the least bit.

Melissa smiled at Samantha. She knew a thing or two about being a rebellious child and she wasn't put off by the frosty reception. "I'm pleased to meet you, too. I'm sorry, everyone, but I've had a long day. I believe I would like to lie down for a while. Samantha, could you show me to my room?"

Samantha glanced at the disapproving adults in the room and wisely chose to comply with Melissa's request. "Sure. It's this way."

Melissa winked at Richard as she walked past him and he nodded. Following Samantha down the hall, Melissa waited until the girl opened the door of a spacious guest room before speaking. "Samantha, can I ask you a favor?"

The girl regarded her with a suspicious frown. "I guess."

"I'd rather you didn't tell your mother this, but I've never babysat before and I have no idea what I'm supposed to do."

"You're kidding, right?"

Melissa sat on the foot of the bed covered with a wedding ring quilt. "Not at all."

"Well, I don't need a babysitter."

"Really? So I'll only have to look after Lauren?"

"I can do that, too."

"Wow, that's a relief."

Samantha propped her hands on her hips. "If you don't know how to babysit, why did you take the job?"

"Because I need a place to live."

"For real?"

"Totally for real. I'm in some trouble and I can't go home. I jumped at the chance to stay here when your uncle offered."

Samantha sat beside Melissa on the bed. "What kind of trouble?"

"I'm not sure you're old enough to know."

"I'll be thirteen in four months."

"I guess that's old enough. The truth is, I'm pregnant and I'm not married. Can I depend on you to help me out with this babysitting stuff? I don't want to freeload on your family. I want to do my share. Is looking after Lauren hard?"

"She's a pain. She'll drive you crazy with all her questions."

"I don't mind that. What will I have to do?"

"You'll have to make sure she eats her breakfast and you really have to get after her to make her brush her teeth before she leaves for school. When she's done in the bathroom, I always check to make sure her toothbrush is wet."

"That doesn't sound too hard. What about after school?"

"You have to make sure she does her homework and chores."

"You've been doing all this when your mother works late? That must put a crimp in your day."

"No kidding. I can't go over to my friend's house.

Ever since the fire, I don't get to do anything but keep an eye on my silly sister."

"If you don't mind, maybe I can help you out."

"I guess that would be okay."

"Really? Because I don't want to step on any toes."

"You need a place to stay and I need a break from Lauren. This could work out good for both of us."

"I hope you're right. Your uncle Richard is a great guy for letting me stay here."

"Yeah, he's pretty cool. Some of my friends think he's the bomb."

Melissa leaned toward Samantha and grinned. "He *is* pretty cute."

Later, after a nap that she honestly did need, Melissa joined Richard's family at the dinner table. She felt awkward and out of place at first, but the feeling soon dissipated.

"I'm in a play at school," Lauren said between bites of pasta salad.

"She's not in the play, she's the *star* of the play," Samantha teased.

"I have the most lines of anybody in my class."

"And we've heard them all fifty times."

"What is your play about?" Melissa intervened before the good-natured squabble could deteriorate.

"It's about the first Thanksgiving. I'm a Wampanoag girl and I show the Pilgrim girls how to make corn cakes and other Indian foods. Massasoit is my father and he is the leader of our tribe."

"Do you show them how to make pecan pie?" Richard asked. "Aunt Lettie says her recipe goes all the way back to colonial times."

"Of course not, silly. They didn't even have pumpkin pie at the first Thanksgiving." Lauren shook her head and rolled her eyes.

Melissa had trouble imagining the redheaded, freckle-faced girl in the part of a Native American.

Angela handed Melissa the basket of rolls. "Try some of these. Dave made them."

Dave gave a hearty guffaw. "With my own two hands, I took the dough out of the freezer and placed them on a cookie sheet."

"That's my style of cooking," Melissa replied. "I'd starve if it weren't for the frozen food section at the grocery store. That and cereal are pretty much my specialties."

Dave grinned and nudged his wife. "Sounds just like you, honey."

She gave him a good-natured swat on the wrist.

Richard asked, "Are you still planning to go back to work at the paper, Melissa?"

She nodded. "I'll be working half days for now until something full-time opens up."

Samantha leaned forward eagerly. "What do you do at the paper? Do you get to photograph crime scenes and dead bodies and interview celebrities?"

Holding back a smile, Melissa said, "I'm a copy girl. I get files for people and hunt up background material for reporters. I answer the phone and take messages. Sometimes I'll go out and pick up photos of people or places that the paper is featuring. I'm afraid it isn't a glamorous job."

Soon talk turned to the progress that was being made on their home, and Melissa listened as both the girls and Angela talked about the changes they wanted made.

Dave listened and nodded and told them if they wanted the place done before Christmas, they would have to stop changing things.

Melissa realized that it was pleasant to be back in the midst of a large and happy family. She hadn't always appreciated her own brothers and sisters, but now that they were all grown-up, she missed the fun they once shared. She glanced at Richard and found him watching her. His smile was warm and friendly and her pulse accelerated. Suddenly afraid that she might actually blush, she looked away.

What was with this sudden attraction to Richard? He had been nothing but kind to her when she was confused and lonely. There couldn't be anything else between them.

Sure she'd had a crush on him, but that had been in high school. He was certainly good-looking enough to make any woman sit up and take notice. His large size, coupled with his gentle nature, would make anyone feel protected, and he had always treated her as an adult, something her parents and her siblings couldn't manage to do, mainly because she was the baby of the family.

When supper ended, Lauren turned to her father. "Dad, will you help me practice my lines for the play?"

"Sure, honey. Let's go in the den."

Samantha looked at her mother. "Veronica Valencia invited me over to listen to her new CDs. Can I go, please?"

Angela shook her head. "It will be too late to go out by the time we get the dishes done."

Samantha looked downcast.

"Let me do these," Melissa offered, gathering up her own plate and silverware. "I've got to start earning my keep sometime. Besides, I'm sure Samantha would rather see her friends than keep me company."

Richard spoke up. "Melissa and I can get the dishes, sis. I know you have things to do."

Angela looked torn. "If you're sure you don't mind. I do have a ton of papers to grade."

"Can I go? Please, Mom?" Samantha pleaded.

"Okay, but don't forget to wear a coat. It looks like it might rain. Be back in an hour."

"Thanks, Mom. Thanks, Melissa." Samantha flashed them both a bright grin, then hurried up the stairs.

With everyone gone their separate ways, the dining room suddenly seemed unnaturally quiet. "You have a terrific family," Melissa told Richard as they carried the plates into the kitchen and stacked them in the sink.

"Thanks. I'm sorry Samantha was rude to you earlier, but she seems to have changed her tune. What did you say to win her over?"

"We talked about a lot of things. Mostly about how unfair it is when you have to take on more responsibility than you're ready for."

"I don't think I understand."

"Samantha wants to help out. She knows how hard things have been, but she misses spending time with her friends and she resents always having to take care of Lauren."

"She told you that?"

"Let's just say I can read between the lines. It wasn't that long ago that I was the baby that none of my siblings had time for. They all wanted to do things I was too young for and if they were watching me, they missed out. And boy, did I hear about it!"

Richard studied her as she rinsed the dishes and handed them to him. She'd caught him by surprise with her astute assessment of Samantha's problem. She had known the girl less than a day and yet she was able to put her finger on the trouble that had been puzzling Angela and Dave for weeks.

"You're amazing."

"Why? Because I know listening to CDs with your girlfriends is more fun than doing dishes with the new sitter? It doesn't take a rocket scientist to figure that one out."

"No, I'm amazed at how perceptive you are. That will certainly help you find the right couple for your baby."

"There is a sobering thought."

"I'm sorry. If you don't want to talk about it, I understand."

"It's not that. It's the idea that I get to choose my child's family. What qualifies me to make that decision? It's not like I've made some first-rate choices so far."

"I think you are being too hard on yourself."

"With an open adoption, does that mean I get to see my baby growing up?"

"It can, but in a limited fashion."

"What if I choose a lousy family? What if I have to watch my child grow up unhappy? Maybe it would be best not to know."

"Melissa, it's normal to have these doubts. I'd be worried if you didn't."

She nodded and handed him another pan for the dishwasher. "Do your sister and her husband know about my…problem?"

"No. I've kept your condition confidential. It's up to you to share what you think they need to know."

"Oh…" She pursed her lips around the drawn-out syllable and regarded him with wide eyes. He was struck by how kissable she looked.

Where had that idea come from? He pushed the disturbing thought aside and said, "What's the matter?"

"I spilled the beans to Samantha, so I think we'd better let Angela and Dave know before they hear it from her."

"Good idea."

"Enough about me. What have you been up to? I meant to tell you that I noticed you've lost some weight. Samantha's girlfriends think you're the bomb."

He was oddly pleased that she had noticed. "What exactly is 'the bomb'?"

"Someone very cool and good-looking."

"Great. I have preteen groupies."

"I'm sure you have groupies in your own age bracket. Tell me the truth, is there someone special?"

He found he didn't mind discussing his disappointments with her. "There was someone a few years ago, but the relationship turned out to be one-sided."

"You fell for her but she didn't fall for you?"

"Something like that. I fell for her and she fell for my best friend."

"Ouch!"

"It turned out for the best. They make a great couple. Besides, I realize now that if she didn't love me, she couldn't be my soul mate. I guess I have to keep looking."

Melissa scrubbed at a spot on one of the plates. "You tell yourself that, but it still hurts when you love someone and they don't love you back."

She was talking about Dean. Richard had the un-Christian notion that he would like to knock some sense into the man, but the thought was quickly followed by the certainty that someday Dean would regret leaving Melissa and their baby.

He said, "It hurts, but that doesn't mean staying together would be better."

"Maybe you're right."

"I get paid to be right."

She giggled. "I forget sometimes that you're my lawyer."

Suddenly, she turned to him, a stunned look on her face. "Oh wow! That means I have to pay you. I never even thought about that."

"I occasionally do *pro bono* cases."

"But that isn't right."

"It's for me to decide if the merits of the case outweigh the money it would earn."

"That's very kind of you, but I can't accept it."

"All right. Then you'll have to wash dishes for months and months to pay off your debt," he said with a smile.

"Be serious, Richard. I can accept a place to live because your sister needs help, but I can't accept your charity."

"If you decide to go through with this adoption—"

"I *am* going though with it," she interjected with force.

"Then you won't have to worry about my fee. The adoptive family normally pays the legal fees."

"I see. Then it's all right, isn't it? Only, promise me one thing. Promise me that you won't let my father pay for anything."

Asking Wallace to help pay Melissa's expenses had been the farthest thing from his mind. Suddenly, he wondered what Wallace would have to say about

Melissa staying here. Of course she was properly chaperoned with his sister and her family living here, but would Wallace see it that way? Or would he think his attorney had gone behind his back to help his wayward daughter instead of sending her home to her mother where she belonged?

The idea was unsettling. He would have to go see Wallace and explain himself. "Have you thought about going to see your father?"

"I've thought about it, but I can't. Maybe once he's home. I can't stand hospitals. They give me the creeps."

"Are you planning a home delivery for your baby?"

"I haven't given it much thought."

"There's a birthing center in Nashville that isn't part of a hospital. You might look into that."

She threw her hands in the air. "Decisions, decisions. That's all everyone wants. Where will I live? Where will I work? Will I give the baby up for adoption or not? I'm sick of making decisions," she said, sniffling.

"Okay." He reached out and drew her into his arms. After a moment, she relaxed against him.

"I'm sorry," she murmured into his shirt front.

"I am, too. Not another single decision tonight."

"Promise?"

"I promise."

"Thank you."

She stepped out of his arms and he missed the warmth of her, missed the feeling of protectiveness she brought out. He knew she was facing the most difficult time of her life. He wanted to ease her way, but he knew that wasn't possible. All he could offer was his friendship.

A few seconds later, Dave came into the kitchen.

"Lauren wants to go out for ice cream. Would you two like to come along? The Cone Shack has twenty-two flavors to choose from."

Richard stole a look at Melissa. The sparkle in her eyes was all it took to send him into a fit of laughter. Melissa tried but couldn't choke back her mirth. Soon they were both laughing like fools.

Dave stood in the doorway looking at them as if they were crazy.

Chapter Six

The next morning, Melissa paused outside the Hamilton Media building, knowing that all eyes would be on her when she entered. No doubt speculation had run rampant among the employees when she had disappeared without a word. Some of the staff were sure to feel resentment that she still had a job after skipping out for five months. She would simply have to tough it out. She was a Hamilton. She could stand up to a few whispers and snide remarks. She was here to work now, and everyone, including her siblings, would soon see that she meant to do a good job.

Fighting back the urge to turn tail and run, she took a deep breath.

"One small step at a time, girl," she whispered. Pasting a smile on her face, she pushed open the revolving front door.

Seated at their posts behind a small reception desk in the lobby were the Gordons. The elderly couple had been with Hamilton Media since ages before Melissa was born. Long since retired from their official jobs, they had become the gatekeepers of the office building. Although they were stooped and gray haired, the Gordons were nothing less than formidable. No outsider made it past their watchful eyes without an appointment.

Melissa's heels tapped lightly on the polished marble floor as she crossed the lobby. Mr. Gordon rose from his seat behind the desk.

"Miss Melissa, it's good to see you again."

"It's nice to be back, Mr. Gordon. Mrs. Gordon, how are you?"

"I'm fine, dear, thank you for asking." She raised the receiver of the phone on the desk. "Will you be wanting to see Miss Amy or Mr. Timothy?"

"Tim, please." Melissa kept moving toward the elevator. If there was one thing Herman and Louise Gordon loved more than their jobs, it was gossip. She didn't intend to give them a chance to begin quizzing her.

"I'll let him know you're on your way up," Thelma said.

Mr. Gordon crossed to the elevator and pushed the up button. Melissa thanked him, entered the old-fashioned dark-paneled lift and waited for the door to close. It took forever. Whatever the Gordons were thinking, they were too polite and too dedicated to the Hamilton family to express a negative opinion by even so much as a raised eyebrow as they regarded her with polite smiles. She smiled back. The doors finally closed seconds before Melissa thought her face would crack.

The lift jerked once, then began its slow climb. The corporate offices were on the third floor.

Step One out of the way. Step Two would be walking into Tim's office and facing him for the first time since she had returned to Davis Landing. The brass doors of the elevator slid open at last and Melissa walked toward her brother's office.

She paused beside the desk of his assistant, Dawn Leroux. Dawn smiled and pointed to the boardroom. "He's waiting for you."

Wondering why Tim had chosen the large meeting room instead of his office, Melissa nodded her thanks and pushed open the heavy walnut door. Tim was seated at the head of the long conference table in the center of the room. Around the table sat her siblings. Only Jeremy was absent. The butterflies in her stomach took a nosedive.

Chris, who was seated closest at the foot of the table, waved a hand toward a chair. "Don't stand there gawking, come in."

Melissa stepped into the room. "I expected to run into the others today, but I didn't expect to see you. Shouldn't you be out arresting bad guys?"

He rose to his feet. "I caught them all last night so I'm taking the day off." He closed the distance between them and wrapped her in a bear hug.

He whispered, "I thought I'd better come see you before you decided to disappear again."

"I'm not going anywhere. I'm home to stay."

He patted her back and stepped away. "I'm glad to hear that."

"So are the rest of us," Amy added, coming to stand beside Melissa.

"We want you to know that we are here for you," Heather chimed in.

Melissa accepted Heather's hug then wiped at the

tears forming in the corners of her eyes. "Thank you. I wasn't expecting this kind of reception."

Tim, impeccable as always in his finely tailored suit, came to stand directly in front of Melissa. "It was Heather's idea and a good one. This family has seen its share of crises in the past few months. It has prompted all of us to do some soul-searching. I, for one, have had the Lord open my eyes to how important my family is to me. We want you to know that whatever it takes, we will help you through this."

"I don't know what to say."

Pulling her into his embrace, he kissed her forehead. "You don't have to say anything, shrimp. Just know that we're your family and we love you."

"Does this mean you forgive me for flushing your baseball cards down the toilet when I was six?"

Everyone laughed, including Tim. He held her at arm's length. "Absolutely not. Do you know what my Willie Mays rookie card would be worth today?"

"More than the package of gum it came in?"

"A lot more."

"Y'all have blown me away. Amy, you had to have a hand in this."

"I knew you were coming back to work today. Heather and I thought it would be best to have everyone meet away from prying eyes."

"Thank you, all of you, for your support. I haven't done much except add to the family's troubles over the past few years, but I'm going to turn over a new leaf."

"Does this mean you won't superglue my favorite running shoes to my closet floor again?" Chris asked with a grin.

"Your shoes are safe, I promise. Now your gun and holster—maybe not."

"That sounds like the pain-in-the-neck kid sister I know."

Melissa turned to his twin. "Heather, you look great. I love what you've done with your hair."

Always the shy one, Heather blushed and tucked a strand of her feathered cut behind her ear.

"I understand congratulations are in order for both you and Chris. I go away for a few months and look what happens."

Melissa spent a few minutes hearing the details of her siblings' engagements, but it wasn't long before Tim took control of the assembly. "Let's everyone have a seat," he suggested. He held out Melissa's chair until she was seated, then took his place at the head of the table again.

Melissa faced her siblings for the first time in years without feeling unhappy or out of place. The words came much easier than she had expected only twenty minutes ago.

"I know that Amy has told all of you that I'm pregnant. Amy, I'm still miffed about that, by the way."

"You'll get over it."

Melissa chuckled. "I'm sure I will."

"What are your plans?" Heather asked gently.

"That's a hard question to answer. I guess the best way to say this is to tell you that I want to find a good home for this baby with a loving couple."

"Adoption?" Chris's voice revealed his surprise.

"Yes. I've made a pretty good mess of my life. I have some work to do on me before I try raising a baby."

Tim clasped his fingers together on the table in front of him. "Are you sure this is what you want?"

"It will be best for both of us in the long run. Mom knows, but I haven't told Dad. I'm hoping none of you will say anything to him until I've had a chance to tell him this myself."

Her family glanced at each other and seemed to reach the same decision. Tim spoke first. "I don't like keeping things from Dad, but I agree that you should be the one to tell him. Are you planning to see him soon?"

"I want to wait until he's out of the hospital."

Heather spoke up. "Dad's doctor says he should be able to come home before Thanksgiving. That's at least two or three weeks."

"I realize that I'm asking a lot, but please do this for me."

Each of her sisters and then her brothers nodded in turn. "It's agreed, then," Tim said. "We'll keep your pregnancy quiet until you've spoken to Dad. Now, what about your job?"

"I understand my old position is still available. I'm ready to get back to work. I also understand that you've kept my insurance paid up. Thanks for that."

"Dad insisted," Tim said. "Where are you living?"

"I'm staying with Richard McNeil and his family for a few weeks, until I can find a place of my own."

Tim frowned at her. "With Richard? Why?"

"His sister needs someone to help with her children for a few weeks. Richard was kind enough to think of me."

"Why don't you move home?" Heather coaxed. "You know you are always welcome."

"I know that, but it's time I stopped relying on Mom

and Dad to bail me out. Now, I want to hear more about these weddings."

Both her sisters were eager to oblige. After listening to them happily discussing wedding plans, bridesmaid dresses and reception dinners, Melissa knew she'd been right not to move home. Her condition and pending adoption would certainly cast a pall over the house.

After a final round of hugs and well-wishing from her family, Melissa followed Tim to the ground floor. They passed the Gordons with nods of acknowledgment and went through the swinging doors to the heart of the *Davis Landing Dispatch,* the newsroom. Although the room still sported the high, hammered tin ceilings of the original structure, the work areas were ultramodern with a maze of half-walled cubicles surrounding computer stations.

Tim escorted her to her desk, in part, she was sure, to show everyone he supported her return.

"Ed Bradshaw knows you're back, Melissa. He'll expect you to do a good job and so will I."

Ed was the managing editor for the paper and a tough but fair man. "Thanks, Tim. I won't let you down."

The phone rang and she snatched up the receiver. "*Davis Landing Dispatch,* Melissa Hamilton speaking. How may I help you?"

Later that afternoon, Melissa used the key Richard had given her to open his front door. She had only a few minutes before the girls were due home from school and she really needed some downtime. Slipping into the quiet house, she kicked off her shoes in the entryway and gave a sigh of relief. "Note to self. Buy sensible shoes for work."

She dropped her purse near her shoes and tossed her coat over the back of the closest chair. It hung for a moment, then slid in a heap to the floor. That was exactly what she felt like—a heap of worn-out fabric.

She laid her folder of papers on the coffee table then she sank onto the sofa. Closing her eyes, she leaned her head back. This was pure bliss. Two seconds later the front door flew open as Lauren and Samantha came in, obviously in the middle of an argument.

"Lauren, you are such a dork."

"Hey, Mom said you can't call me that."

"Dork, dork, dork!"

Melissa sat up straight as the girls entered the room. "Is this the part where I get to tell you girls what to do?"

"Melissa, tell her she can't call me a dork."

"Samantha, don't call your sister a dork."

"Tell her not to act like a dork."

"Lauren, do as you sister says and don't act like a dork."

"Hey, that's not fair!"

"Told you she'd side with me."

Melissa held up one hand. "Stop. Pretend I've walked into the movie ten minutes late. In five words or less, tell me what started this."

Lauren came and dropped onto the sofa beside Melissa. "She's mad because I told Bobby Lambert she likes him."

"That was more than five words, but I get the picture. Samantha?"

"I've never been so humiliated in my life." Samantha took off her backpack and sat down on the other side of Melissa.

One look at Samantha's face was all Melissa needed. "I take it that you do like this boy?"

Lauren scooted forward to look at her sister around Melissa. "Of course she likes him. She wrote his name in her diary about a hundred times—with little hearts around it."

Outraged, Samantha sat forward and glared at her sister. "You read my diary?"

"You left it lying open on the bed. I couldn't miss it."

"Brat! I'll be *so* glad to get my own room again."

"Okay, girls, stop it. Lauren, you need to apologize to your sister. Even if she left her diary open, you know that what she wrote was private and you had no right to read it or repeat it. Especially to the person she wrote about. Answer me honestly, you knew it would make her mad, didn't you?"

Flopping back, Lauren crossed her arms. "Yes."

"Tell me why you would do such a thing."

"Because she was making fun of my part in the play in front of everybody."

Feeling much more like her own mother than Melissa had ever thought possible, she turned to Samantha. "Did you make fun of your sister?"

"All she does is talk about her role in that stupid play."

"It's not a stupid play!"

"Of course it isn't." Melissa tried to soothe hurt feelings.

"She said I couldn't play a Native American because they don't have freckles."

Since Melissa previously had had the same thought about Lauren's red hair and Irish looks, she refrained from commenting.

"Samantha's just mad because I got chosen to be in the play and she didn't get chosen to be in the junior choir at church."

Samantha's chin came up. "Who cares about the dumb old choir? I only wanted to be in it because Bobby is."

Melissa slipped her arm around Samantha. "I'm sorry. I didn't know you sang. That must have been disappointing."

"They're just a bunch of losers, anyway."

"I'm sure that isn't true, but do the two of you see what you are doing to each other?"

Samantha glared at her out from beneath her bangs. "What?"

"Your feelings were hurt by losing out on a position in the singing group. It's okay to be upset about that, but you shouldn't have taken it out on your sister. And Lauren, what Samantha said was hurtful, but it wasn't right to try and hurt her back by revealing what was in her diary. You both need to apologize. There isn't anything as important as your family." That was a lesson Melissa had learned the hard way.

"I know," Lauren admitted. "I'm sorry, Samantha."

"I'm sorry I made fun of your part in the play."

"That's better. Samantha, I know a little something about singing. I took lessons when I was younger. My ex-boyfriend was in a band. The guy who sang the vocals used to practice and I'd play the scales for him on the keyboard. I'd be happy to help you work on your voice."

"Really? Nah, I don't think that will help. I stink."

"Lauren, is she any good?"

Lauren peeked at Samantha. "She's okay."

"I'm better than okay!"

"What did the choir director say about your voice?"

"He said I didn't project."

"Oh, that's an easy thing to fix. I can help you do that."

"You can?" Samantha began to look interested.

"Sure. I'll show you some exercises now, if you like. Unless you want to go to Veronica's house? Your mother said it would be all right as long as I checked with Veronica's mother first."

"I can see her at school tomorrow. I have a keyboard in my room."

"Great. Lauren, what are your plans?"

"I've got math homework. I can do it down here at the table while Samantha sings. Her screeching won't bother me if you keep the door shut."

Melissa ruffled Lauren's curly hair. "We'll keep it down to a dull roar. Come and get me if you need help with your homework."

Melissa and Samantha rose to leave the room, but Lauren called after her, "Melissa, don't you think you should pick up your things? Mom says we have to keep Uncle Richard's house neat."

Melissa glanced at her scattered trail from the doorway to the sofa. "You're right. Hey, who is the grown-up here?" Reaching down, she grabbed Lauren's sides and tickled her until they both dissolved into a fit of giggles.

From the doorway of his office just off the family room, Richard listened with amazement and a measure of pride to the way Melissa handled his nieces. She might believe she didn't have what it takes to be a mother, but he had to disagree. She was selling herself short. She certainly seemed to have a knack for dealing with kids.

Perhaps she would change her mind and keep her baby.

With a self-deprecating shake of his head, he stepped back inside his office. He had no business having an opinion on the subject one way or the other. That was Melissa's decision.

He returned to his desk. Picking up the phone, he placed the call he had been thinking about making when he'd heard the girls come home. On the second ring his friend picked up.

"Melbourne Adoption agency, Jake Melbourne speaking."

"Jake, this is Richard McNeil."

"Richard, it's good to hear your voice. How are you?"

"I'm fine, Jake. Have you got a few minutes?"

"For you, always."

"I have a young woman who is considering placing her child for adoption and I was wondering if you could handle the placement."

"Of course. You know we always have dozens of couples on our waiting list."

"The young woman is a friend and I want to make sure things go smoothly. I'd like to stay involved, if that's okay."

"I understand. Why don't I send over our information packet, a photo album of couples and their 'Dear Birth Mom' letters? That should give your friend an idea of how we operate."

"Sounds good."

"Has she been to see a doctor recently?"

"I don't think so. She's only just arrived in town."

"She should do that first. We often send our girls to Dr. Kathy Miller. I can set up an appointment. She makes a point of seeing patients from us on short notice."

"That would be fine. Let me know when and I'll see that she gets there."

"Audrey was saying just the other day that we haven't seen you in ages. Why don't you come over for dinner one of these nights?"

For the first time since their wedding three years before, Richard found himself looking forward to spending time with his best friend and his wife. The pain of losing Audrey to Jake had faded to a dull ache over time, but it seemed his wounded heart was truly healed, at last. When had that happened?

After Melissa came back to town, he realized with a sense of wonder. He said, "I'd like that. Tell Audrey I said hello and give her my love."

Tuesday morning, Melissa called a cab as soon as the girls were out the door to school and arrived at work a few minutes early. Throughout the morning, she filed reports, answered phone calls and ran errands. A little after noon, Ed Bradshaw stopped at her desk.

"Melissa, I need this file taken over to Central Tennessee University right away. Felicity is doing a story on a new program there and she needs this information for her interview with the dean."

"I'm sorry, Mr. Bradshaw, but I don't have a car."

"I don't have anyone else I can send right now. Take a cab and charge it to the office."

"Yes, sir."

File in hand, Melissa gladly escaped from her desk and enjoyed the ride out to the university. Stepping out of the cab in front of the campus's main building, she took a deep breath of the crisp fall air. The private college with its ivy-covered brick building and spacious lawns was a much better place to spend the afternoon than inside her cubicle.

Students with books clutched in their arms criss-crossed the green grass. Others were seated on benches and walls taking advantage of the lingering warmth of the day. The tall oak and sycamore trees that dotted the grounds had begun losing their colorful leaves in gentle cascades as the breeze stirred them.

With the help of a friendly receptionist, she was able to locate Felicity Simmons in a small waiting room outside the dean's office. Besides being a beautiful and intelligent woman, as well as a fine reporter, Felicity also happened to be engaged to Melissa's brother, Chris. Not knowing how much, if anything, Chris had shared about her situation, Melissa approached her with some trepidation.

"Miss Simmons, I've brought the file you need."

Felicity swept her reddish hair back and looked up from her notepad. Her bright smile instantly set Melissa at ease.

"Melissa, how nice to see you. Chris told me you were back, but I haven't had time to stop by and say hello."

"I'm the one who should be apologizing. I haven't yet said congratulations on your engagement. Chris is a fortunate man."

"Thank you. Sit down, please." She gestured toward a brown leather chair beside hers.

Eager to stay away from talk of the family, Melissa asked, "What story are you covering?"

"The university is opening a new work study program for single parents. Since this is a private college, the program will begin as a two-year pilot. After that, I understand the plan is to reevaluate and see if they can make it a permanent part of the curriculum. It will take a long-term financial commitment from the school, but the women that qualify will be able to attend classes for free or at a very reduced fee while they work here."

"That's wonderful."

"It is. So many young women aren't able to continue their education because of the high cost of college. Their only option is to stay in a low-paying job because it puts food on the table. This program is aimed at breaking the cycle of poverty for them."

"So this is just for single mothers?"

"That's one of the questions I need answered today. I'd like to make sure that single fathers aren't being excluded."

The dean's receptionist hung up her phone and came around the desk. "Miss Simmons, Dean Bailey is ready to see you now."

"Thank you." Felicity turned to Melissa. "Would you like to sit in on the interview?"

"Could I? That would be fabulous."

"Come on. You can be my assistant. Afterward, we'll get a cup of coffee and you can tell me all the crazy things Chris did as a kid that he doesn't want me to know about."

"That'll take more than one cup."

"All right, we'll make it two cups and you can tell me what drives him nuts. It never hurts a woman to have the straight facts about her man."

Chapter Seven

Wednesday evening, the McNeil household was in a state of mild uproar. Melissa sat in the family room watching the latest crime investigation show on TV and tried to stay out of everyone's way. The school play was due to start in an hour.

"Mom, I can't find my moccasins!"

"They're on your bed."

"I looked there."

"Look again."

"Angela, where is my blue tie?" Dave wandered into the family room, parked himself on the arm of the sofa and instantly became engrossed in the television show.

His wife came by a minute later, tie in hand. "Here it is, dear. Dave, don't you dare start watching that show. We have to leave in five minutes or the star of the show will be late."

"Mom, I still can't find my moccasins!" Lauren shouted from the landing.

"Samantha, help your sister find her shoes!" Dave

bellowed, keeping his eyes glued to the set as his wife slipped his tie over his head.

"Never mind, I've got them." Lauren raced into the room, the dark braids of her wig flying out behind her and the fringe of her dress fluttering with every move.

Melissa turned in her chair. "Lauren, you look great."

"Thanks. Hey, why aren't you getting dressed?" A stricken look crossed her young face. "You are coming, aren't you?"

"Tonight is for you and your family. I'm going to stay here and enjoy a quiet night home alone."

"But you can't miss this. You've got to come."

Dave finished adjusting his tie. "You're welcome to come, Melissa. We'd love to have you."

"I'm not ready and I would make you late if you had to wait on me."

"I don't mind waiting until Melissa gets ready. We can take two cars. That way the rest of you won't be late." Richard's deep voice behind her sent an unexpected shiver down her spine.

She looked over her shoulder. "That's okay. Really. I'm sure you want to go with your family."

"Melissa, you have to come. Please?" Lauren pleaded. "You may never, ever, get another chance to see me on stage."

Melissa saw Richard's lips twitch as he held back a smile. "Yes, please come. You don't want to upset our star on her big night, do you?"

"Of course not. All right, I'll come," she answered quickly. She realized she was far too willing to spend any amount of time with Richard, and she hoped he didn't notice her eagerness.

Lauren threw her arms around Melissa. "Yeah! Thank you, thank you. After the play we're going out for supper at my favorite place, the Mexican Hat Café."

"I know the place. They have great food." She cast a sidelong glance at Richard. A play and dinner. It almost felt like a date.

As the family gathered their coats and made their way out the door at last, silence settled over the house.

Richard clapped his hands. "Get a move on, woman."

She jumped up from the sofa. "I'm going, I'm going."

"How long will it take you?"

"Ten minutes tops." She headed for the hall.

"Make it snappy. I'll call my date and tell her I'm going to be a few minutes late, but I warn you, she doesn't like to be kept waiting."

Melissa spun around to stare at him. He was bringing a date? The idea shouldn't have been so startling but it was.

She struggled briefly with a sense of disappointment, then realized her foolishness. He'd said that there wasn't anyone special in his life, not that he didn't date. He was her friend. She had to stop foolishly reading more into his kindness.

Walking back toward him, she said, "I can't intrude on your date, Richard."

"You're not intruding. You were invited."

"No, you go on. I'll be fine here."

"Nonsense. Lauren is expecting you. You can't back out now. Hurry up or we won't get decent seats."

Nodding in reluctant agreement, she did as he asked, but her excitement at being included had fled.

Fifteen minutes later they were threading their way though traffic, headed toward Mill Road Bridge and the town of Hickory Mills. The lights of the city made a festive backdrop beyond the car windows. The holidays were fast approaching. Already many stores had Christmas displays in their windows.

What would her holidays be like this year? Melissa wondered. She dreaded going through Christmas. Each year she marked the anniversary of Jenny's death on December twenty-first, and each year it became harder to find the joy that seemed to possess everyone else during the season.

At least by Christmas she would be able to afford her own place, and she wouldn't inflict her dismal spirits on Richard or her own family. Only, did she really want to spend the holidays alone? Pushing aside her troubling thoughts, she focused on the road ahead. "Does your girlfriend live in Hickory Mills?"

"My what? Oh, you mean my date. Yes, she does. I've been trying to get her to move to our side of the river, but she won't hear of it."

He turned onto the street that ran past the bus station near the downtown area and pulled up beside a dark storefront. On the second story, lights blazed brightly from the tall arched windows that faced the street. His friend must live in a loft apartment.

"I'll be right back," he said opening his door.

Melissa knew a moment of unease as he sprinted up the stairs to the second-floor landing. What would his date think about him showing up with another woman in tow? The last thing Melissa wanted to do was cause problems for the man who had befriended her. A few minutes later, Richard emerged from the stairwell with a small, white-haired woman clinging to his arm.

Escorting her to the car, he opened the back door, but she said, "Oh, don't make me sit in the back seat like somebody's granny. I can't hear a thing anyone says back there. I'll sit up front if your young lady doesn't mind." She leaned down and wagged her fingers at Melissa.

"Of course, I don't mind. I'll be glad to sit in the rear," Melissa assured her. She gathered her purse and opened her door, but the elderly woman was beside her before she could climb out.

"You don't want to sit in the back by yourself. Scoot over, dearie, there's plenty of room for all of us in this boat."

Melissa quickly found herself sandwiched between Richard's muscular shoulder and the spry little woman who seemed to need more than her fair share of the front seat.

"Introduce me to this lovely girl, Richard."

"I was about to. Melissa Hamilton, meet my great-aunt, Lettie McNeil."

"I'm pleased to meet you, Mrs. McNeil." Melissa extended her hand as well as she could in the cramped quarters. "You must be the pie lady."

Lettie's laugh crackled gleefully. "That would be me. You can call me Lettie, dearie. What a treat she is, Richard. I think she's a keeper. She's not hard on the eyes, either."

"Lettie, Melissa is a family friend." Richard's voice held a playful hint of warning.

"Pshaw, boy, let an old woman dream. Do you bake, child?"

Melissa, more bemused by the second, shook her head.

Lettie patted her arm. "Well, that's okay. I'll be happy

to teach you. A girl can't be thinking about settin' up house unless she can cook."

Melissa sent him a questioning look.

"Ignore her," Richard suggested. "She's gotten a bit daft in her old age."

"I'm not the only one getting older, Richard. Don't go forgetting that fact. Melissa, tell me about yourself. Are you related to the Hamiltons that own the newspaper?"

Richard drove toward the school and listened with amusement to Melissa answering his aunt's rapid-fire questions. Lettie was normally polite to the women he dated when they met, but she was seldom outright charming. He wasn't fooled by her ploy that she couldn't hear in the back seat. The woman's hearing was every bit as good as his, if not better.

Still, he didn't mind the close contact with Melissa. He liked the feel of her snuggled against him. For one heady moment, he considered draping his arm around her, but quickly dismissed the idea. What made him think she would welcome such a gesture from him?

At the school, Lauren's third-grade play went off with only one minor hitch. A nervous pilgrim boy forgot his lines and left the other actors and actresses to flounder briefly. Their teacher, watching from the wings, was able to prompt him and the rest of the play sailed on smoothly.

Throughout the performance, Richard found himself watching Melissa more than the Thanksgiving special. She seemed to be enjoying herself, whispering asides to Lettie and waiting with bated breath each time Lauren recited her lines. He could tell she shared Angela and Dave's pride in their daughter's accomplishments when Lauren's voice rang out sure and precise each time.

Afterward, as the families and friends milled around waiting for the children in the hallway outside the auditorium, Richard took Melissa's elbow to guide her away from a group of jostling youngsters. She smiled her thanks and his heart faltered, then quickened its beat.

It wasn't the first time he had noticed what beautiful eyes she had. They were a luminous, dark, liquid brown and seemed to shine with an inner light when she smiled. He chided himself for acting like a romantic fool. He'd never seen himself as the knight-in-shining-armor type, but he could imagine slaying dragons for this fair young maiden.

"Uncle Richard, did you see me?" Lauren came charging down the hall with one of her fellow actresses at her side.

"I saw you, kiddo. You were great."

"Did you see me, Melissa?"

"Of course I did. You were the perfect Wampanoag girl. Totally believable."

"I was?"

"Absolutely," Melissa assured her.

Pulling her friend forward by the arm, Lauren said, "I want you to meet my very best friend in the whole, wide world. This is Talia Valencia."

Melissa kept a smile on her face, but it was difficult as painful memories overwhelmed her. How many times had she and Jenny introduced themselves in the same manner in this very school building? "My very best friend in the whole, wide world."

Jenny, why did you have to die? You promised we'd be friends forever.

Lauren tugged at her friend's hand. "Come and meet my great-great aunt. She's a hoot."

"It was nice meeting you," Talia called back in Melissa's direction.

Suddenly, Melissa wanted to go home. She wanted to see her old room filled with photos and trinkets that would bring her memories of Jenny into focus. What had their third-grade play been about? What had Jenny been wearing the day she turned sixteen? What did she look like that day? Surly that had to have been one of the best days of their lives. How could she have forgotten? The only image she recalled was of Jenny's face, ghastly pale, her beautiful, dark blond hair only patches of stubble after the chemo. Jenny in the hospital bed, gasping for breath and begging Melissa not to let her die.

The hallway began spinning out of focus. Melissa couldn't catch her breath.

"Melissa, are you all right?"

Jerked out of the past, Melissa clutched Richard's arm to steady herself. "I need some air."

"Of course." He slipped an arm around her waist and half supported her as he led her toward the school doors and out into the chilly night. She drew in deep, ragged breaths as she leaned on him and clutched his suit jacket in her hands.

"Melissa, you're scaring me. What's wrong? Is it the baby?"

"I'm fine. I just need a minute." Already the terrible memory was fading. She willed it to the dark place in the back of her mind.

"Maybe I should see if there's a doctor here?"

"Don't go shouting, 'Is there a doctor in the house?'

Please, I'll be fine in a minute." Her laugh was shaky, but it seemed to reassure him. The panic left his eyes, but his concern remained.

"I won't yell for a doctor if you're sure you're all right. You went as pale as a sheet in there."

"I'm sorry. It must have been the crowd." She wasn't going to dredge those memories up by talking about them now. Little by little, she began to realize she was being held in Richard's arms—and it felt wonderful. He seemed so strong and yet so tender. He was a buffer between her and the sadness that threatened to overwhelm her. He made her feel comforted, protected—safe. If only those feelings could last.

She tried to pull away. His arm tightened. "Let's find a place to sit down first."

He led her across a small strip of lawn to where a low brick wall ringed the flagpole. Only when she was seated did his hold on her loosen. She shivered, more from the loss of his embrace than from the cool night air, but he quickly pulled off his jacket and wrapped her in it. It wasn't as good as his arms, but it carried the scent of his masculine aftershave and she snuggled deeper into its warmth.

He sat beside her and with a gentle hand to her chin he turned her face toward the light coming from the school. She managed a weak smile. "I'm sorry I scared you."

"I'm sorry I insisted you come tonight. You would have been better off resting at home."

"And miss Lauren's big night? No, it would take more than a dizzy spell to make me regret coming."

How can I be sorry you held me in your arms? For a second she was afraid she had said the words aloud.

"Are you sure the baby is okay?"

She pressed her hand to her tummy. There was no thumping going on, but she felt fine. "I'm sure."

"Thank the Lord."

She was astonished at the degree of relief in those three words. A flush of tenderness filled her heart. He really was concerned about her child. She found the thought endearing. The contrast between the way he behaved and the way Dean had acted was as different as day and night.

"There you are, sitting in the dark like a pair of spooning sweethearts," Lettie called out as she came across the grass, a mischievous smile twitching at the corner of her mouth.

Richard rolled his eyes and Melissa smothered a nervous giggle.

"Shall I try and explain?" he asked under his breath.

"No, let the old woman dream," Melissa whispered back.

Maybe, just maybe, a young woman could dream, too.

Later, after she had reassured him for the fifteenth time that she was fine, Richard reluctantly agreed to let her join the rest of the family for supper at their favorite restaurant. He kept a close eye on her and barely noticed what he ordered or the bright Mexican decor. What he wanted to do was take Melissa home and wrap her in cotton wool. She had scared the daylights out of him. Now, she sat talking to Samantha and Lauren as if nothing had happened.

As if his heart hadn't plummeted to the pit of his stomach at the sight of her pale face. As if the scent of her perfume didn't still cling to his jacket and stir the memory of her slender form enfolded in his arms. As if the smiles he coaxed from her didn't make him feel like a prince. If nothing had happened, why did he find himself staring at her like a lovesick schoolboy?

She leaned toward him and gestured toward his plate. "How are the cheese enchiladas? I thought you'd like them. They are one of my favorite dishes from here."

"They're fine." He couldn't think of anything else to say. The riot of emotions filling his mind left him tongue-tied.

She took another sip of her iced tea, then dunked a chip into the salsa. "I've always liked this place. The food is so authentic."

Angela motioned toward Richard's plate with her fork. "Those aren't on your diet, are they? You know what the doctor said."

Concern dimmed the happiness in Melissa's eyes as she stared at him. "What doctor? Richard, are you sick?"

"His cholesterol was sky-high," Angela answered before he could say anything.

"It's under control now," he interjected.

"He has to watch his stress and his diet. Our dad died of a heart attack when he was only forty-eight. With a family history like that, Richard's doctor is keeping a close eye on him. Richard knows what he's facing. He has to take care of himself."

Richard could have cheerfully strangled his sister. The last thing Melissa needed was someone else to worry about. He sought to reassure her. "I do watch what I eat, and I jog four miles three times a week."

Melissa didn't look the least bit reassured. Frowning,

she reached over and snatched his plate away. "I wish I had known. I never would have suggested you try these. Here, have my salad. I haven't touched it."

Across the way, Lettie propped her elbow on the table and winked at him. "She sounds just like a wife, doesn't she? That's what you need, Richard, a sensible wife to look after you."

Beside her, Lauren brightened. "Hey, Melissa could marry Uncle Richard and be his wife. Then she wouldn't have to move out when we leave and we could come and see her anytime we wanted. What do you think?"

Melissa ducked her head and he couldn't see her face. Around him, the others laughed. All except Aunt Lettie, who watched both of them with keen interest.

Chapter Eight

The next morning, Richard decided to pay an overdue visit to Wallace Hamilton at Community General. The new medical center, a modern glass-and-steel building, was only a few blocks from the downtown area, so he didn't have to travel far out of his way.

As he walked down the austere, brightly lit corridor toward Wallace's room, Richard went over in his mind the things he needed to say and the things that would be better left unsaid until Melissa found the courage to face her father.

That she hadn't been to see her father already troubled Richard deeply. He prayed daily for her to find the spiritual and emotional strength she needed. The other thing troubling him was his growing attraction to her. It was difficult to believe she had only been back in town a week. During that short space of time he found himself thinking of her as more than a friend, but he realized that his timing couldn't have been worse. She was in the midst of a personal crisis, and he certainly didn't want to add to her burden.

The door to Wallace's room stood open. The silver-haired patriarch of the Hamilton family was sitting up in bed. Once a dynamic and active man, Wallace's illness had taken its toll. Today, he looked much older than his fifty-nine years. His normally tanned complexion held a sallow color that clashed with the navy-blue silk pajamas he wore. An IV pole on the far side of the bed held a unit of blood that dripped slowly into the catheter in his left arm. Richard knocked softly.

Wallace looked toward the door and his face brightened. "Richard, what are you doing here? Come in."

"I just stopped by to see if you were up to a round of golf?"

"I'd take you up on the offer if it weren't for this blasted contraption they've got hooked to me. They stick needles in me to draw blood for tests and then the tests tell them I need more blood. If they'd leave what I've got in me, I wouldn't need this stuff."

Richard sat in the green vinyl recliner beside the bed and loosened his tie with one hand. It was obvious Wallace wasn't having one of his good days.

"Are you here to tell me Tim has run the company into the ground?"

Shaking his head, Richard said, "Tim is doing a fine job with the company. You can rest easy about that."

"Rest is all I get to do. But try spending a few months in this place and you'll find they never let you rest easy. Some fool nurse is always coming in to check my temperature. Who cares at one o'clock in the morning?"

"Maybe I should come back another time."

"No, don't go. I'm cranky and sick and tired of being here. I thought once I licked the leukemia with this bone marrow transplant I'd be up and around in no time. I never expected a little fungus to lay me low."

"A fungal infection is a very serious complication, Wallace. You have to give the drugs time to work."

"That's what Dr. Strickland tells me."

"You should listen to him."

"I know, I know. Now you sound like Nora. If you didn't come to listen to me complain, why are you here?"

"Can't I come to visit an old friend?"

"Not with that worried frown making a crease between your eyes. What's on your mind? Out with it."

"I've come about Melissa."

"What's that ungrateful daughter of mine done now? Her mother told me she was back in town."

"I don't think Melissa is ungrateful, Wallace. I think she's simply struggling to find herself."

"That's a euphemism for flighty if I've ever heard one. She hasn't come to see me, you know. Not once since I've been in here. Wouldn't you call that ungrateful?" While he tried to hide it with his gruff words, Richard could see Wallace was truly wounded by the fact that his daughter hadn't visited.

"I don't know where we went wrong with that child. I tell you, this last stunt was the icing on the cake—taking off with that low-life boyfriend of hers. It won't take much more to make me wash my hands of her for good."

Richard chose his next words carefully. It was apparent that Wallace was working himself into a state. "Melissa is trying to turn her life around. She's back working at the paper and she's helping my sister with her girls. It isn't easy for her, but she's trying."

Wallace scowled at him. "You seem to know a lot more about what my daughter is up to than I do."

"I'm afraid that's true. She was wanting a place to stay and I offered her a room at my place. Before you go off the deep end, I want to make it clear that Angela, Dave and the girls are there as chaperones. Melissa is earning her room and board—it isn't charity. She wants to make it on her own, without your help."

"If she hates being a Hamilton so much, let her see how hard it is to earn a living without her old man's money to fall back on or to bail her out when she gets in debt. She can mooch off you, I don't care. But mark my words, when you least expect it, she'll take off with some new boyfriend without so much as a note."

"I don't think that's going to happen. I think she really is determined to start over."

"I'll believe it when I see it."

"All right. I wanted you to know she was staying someplace safe and for you not to worry."

"She should be with her mother. There's the person who worries about her. If you want to help Melissa, convince her to go home."

"I've tried. The problem is, she's as stubborn as her old man."

"Humph!" For a second, Richard thought he saw a flicker of pride in her father's eyes, but just as quickly it was gone.

Rising to his feet, Richard laid a hand on Wallace's shoulder. "I've got to get into the office. Margaret will have the police looking for me if I'm late. It was good seeing you, sir. I look forward to the day when I can beat you soundly in a good round of golf."

"Beat me? That'll be the day. You'd better get some practice in while I'm laid up."

"I have been. I went four under par at Lark Meadows two weeks ago."

"Brag when you've beaten my six under par."

"You'd better believe I will. Take care, sir."

As he reached the door, Wallace called out, "Richard?"

He paused and looked back. "Yes?"

"Keep an eye on her for me."

"I will, sir. Goodbye."

After spending the rest of the day in a fruitless attempt to work, Richard gave in and sent his secretary home early. The unexpected time off surprised Margaret so much that she offered to make an appointment with his doctor right away. She was sure he must be coming down with something. He was, but it wasn't anything his doctor could fix. He was coming down with a case of severe infatuation with Melissa Hamilton.

When his secretary was gone, Richard turned in his chair to face the window and looked out over the treetops in the park across the street. From here, he could just make out the flag fluttering in the breeze on the other side of Sugar Tree Park at the town's elementary school. Sitting on the low wall by the flagpole was the last place he had expected to find himself struggling against the desire to kiss one wayward young woman.

It had been a long time since he had found himself this attracted to someone. Only Melissa wasn't just any woman. For one thing, she was his client. That alone made any relationship with her a violation of his professional ethics, only it seemed that knowing she was off-limits and getting her out of his mind were two entirely different problems. If only he could put his finger on what it was about her that intrigued him.

He was used to looking at a problem from all angles, locating the best way to solve it and then presenting a sound case to his clients. Melissa didn't fit into any of the categories he normally assigned the women in his life. His feelings for her were much too strong to dismiss as friendship, but he certainly couldn't be falling in love with her.

The idea was ridiculous. She was too young, for one thing. She wasn't committed to her faith or to serving her community. She was carrying another man's child. What he should feel was pity. It was painfully obvious that she was adrift in life, but pity wasn't what stirred his heart when she was near. What stirred his heart was the flowerlike scent of her hair, and the humor that sparkled in the depths of her eyes whenever she made light of her troubles. It was the conviction in her voice when she spoke about starting her life over. It was the kindness and joy she shared so easily with his family.

Face it, man, it's everything about her.

He disliked the idea that he wasn't in control of his own emotions. He might have been able to keep on believing he was—until last night. Last night, when she had taken his unhealthy dinner from him and given him her salad instead, she had touched his heart. She cared about him.

The hard truth was that he just might be falling in love. The only question that remained unanswered was, what should he do about it?

The answer was clear, even if he didn't like it. There was nothing to be done. Melissa was off-limits as long as she was staying under his roof and as long as he was her attorney.

* * *

Later that night, after dinner was finished and the girls had gone to bed, Richard walked into the family room and found Melissa reading. "Could I speak to you for a few minutes?"

She put down the medical encyclopedia she held. "Sure. What's up?"

"This discussion might be better in my office."

"Sounds like I'm in trouble."

"Not at all. Come on. I keep a stash of jelly beans in there. I'll share, but don't tell the girls."

"Are those on your diet?"

"Yup. Zero fat."

"I'll have to look that up. I've been researching what kinds of food you should have. Diet and exercise may not be enough. Sometimes you have to take cholesterol-lowering drugs."

"Yes, my doctor discussed that with me."

"Good." She rose and headed down the hall to his study.

He followed her inside and took a seat in one of the dark brown leather wingback chairs that flanked a small brick fireplace. The gentle glow from the burning gas logs in the arched hearth added a homey touch to the room. Paneled in dark wood with built-in floor-to-ceiling bookshelves across one wall, the room was his favorite spot in the house. Since Angela and her family had moved in, he used it more as a quiet place to retreat and read or listen to music rather than a place to work.

"So what did you want to talk to me about?"

Was it his imagination, or did she seem uneasy with his company tonight?

"A couple of things. First, my friend who runs the

adoption agency has made an OB appointment for you."
He pulled a card from his pocket and handed it to her.

"All right. What else?"

"I went to see your father today."

"You didn't tell him I was pregnant, did you?"

He sought to calm her sudden alarm. "Of course not.
I merely told him that you were living here."

She looked down and rubbed her palms on the fabric
of her cream-colored corduroy pants. She wore a loose
blouse with thin green stripes that reminded him of
fresh mint.

"How is Daddy?"

"Tired. Cranky. He was getting another transfusion."

She looked up and he saw deep concern in her eyes.
"I thought his leukemia was under control."

"This infection he's fighting has weakened his system."

"But he's going to be all right, isn't he?"

"The doctors are doing everything they can. Melissa,
you should go see him."

"I know. I will. When I'm ready."

"Ready for what?"

She sprang to her feet and faced the fire, holding her
hands to the warmth. "You know how he is. Nothing
I do or say is going to be good enough to please him.
He already thinks my life is one big effort to spite
him. He'll be sure of that when I tell him about my
pregnancy."

"Your father loves you."

She gave him a wry smile over her shoulder. "Yeah,
but he doesn't like me much."

"You need to give him a chance to see that you've
changed."

"Have I?"

"I think you have. I see a much more mature woman than the one I knew five months ago."

"Finding yourself broke, pregnant and alone in a strange city can do that." She turned to face him. "I am trying to make the right choices now, but I know what will happen when I see Daddy. He'll make me feel lower than the dust under the rug without even trying. He'll give me that look, and I'll know that no matter what I say or do, he's already disappointed. He'll make me want to cut and run. I'm not strong enough to see him yet."

"I think you are."

She turned back to the fire, crossing her arms in front of her. "Thanks for the vote of confidence, but I'm a yellow-bellied coward. I need more time."

"You're harder on yourself than anyone else will be."

"Know why?"

"Why?"

"Because I've tried a thousand times to be the daughter he wants and I've failed a thousand times. After a record like that, a person quits trying. Then quitting gets easier and easier."

"Have you considered the fact that you failed because you can't do it alone?"

"Is this the part where you tell me God can help?" she scoffed.

"If you never forgive yourself for failing, Melissa, how will you allow others to forgive you?"

She gave him a hard stare over her shoulder. "What do you mean?"

"'Love thy neighbor as thyself' is a two-way street.

You have to love yourself in order to love others. When you realize that, you will find the strength you need."

"I'm sorry. I didn't mean to mock your beliefs, Richard."

"My beliefs can't be altered by anyone's mockery. They go too deep for that."

She returned to her chair, sitting on the edge as she leaned toward him with her elbows propped on her knees and her hands clasped before her. "How did you find such faith?"

"How did you lose yours? You used to go to church with your family. I remember seeing you there."

"You're right. I went to church when I was younger. I believed. But I didn't turn my back on God. He turned His back on me."

"Tell me what happened."

"I don't feel like talking about this. Please, excuse me." She rose from her chair and started for the door, but Richard stopped her with a hand on her arm.

"Don't run away."

"Didn't you know? It's what I do best." Her sarcasm didn't quite cover the pain in her voice.

"But it's not what you want to do. Talking can help. Honestly."

She hesitated, and he was afraid she would leave. He wanted to help her, to understand her.

With a ragged sigh, she nodded. He dropped his hands and shoved them in the front pockets of his jeans. Mainly because he wanted to wrap them around Melissa and hold her close. He wanted to offer her the comfort of his embrace, but he sensed she didn't need that now. She needed to find a way to tell her story in her own words.

She moved again to stand in front of the fireplace with her arms crossed as if huddling against the cold—or against her memories. "You remember Jennifer Wilson, don't you?"

"Of course. She was a neighbor of yours."

"She was more than my next-door neighbor. Jenny was my best friend from the time I could walk. We were inseparable. I was closer to her than to any of my sisters, even."

"She died several years ago, am I correct?"

Melissa nodded. Looking into the flames, she could almost see Jenny's bright smile, almost hear her laughter. "She became sick when we were juniors in high school, non-Hodgkin's lymphoma. From its name, you would think it's better than having Hodgkins, but it isn't. It's worse."

"That must have been a sad time for you."

A shiver ran up her spine. It had been much more than a sad time. Even now, it was difficult to put into words the way she felt back then.

"From the day Jenny was diagnosed, we never did anything together again. She had chemo and radiation. She took drugs that made her hair fall out. They were supposed to help her, but they didn't. She threw up all the time and lost weight. Each day I saw her slipping further away. I never understood why it happened to her and not to me. We shared everything. We had the chicken pox at the same time. If one of us had a cold, the other was sure to get it, too."

"It's normal to feel guilty about being well when someone you love is sick."

"There's nothing normal about a sixteen-year-old

girl wasting away in front of your eyes because her own body has decided to kill her."

"Is that when you lost faith in God?"

"What kind of God does such a horrible thing? I prayed for Jenny. I got down on my knees every night and I prayed for her to get well. I prayed and God turned a deaf ear." She didn't want to talk about this anymore. Why was he probing into old wounds? What did he want from her?

"Just because your prayer wasn't answered the way you wanted, it doesn't mean God wasn't listening."

"Oh, I know He wasn't listening. I was with Jenny the day she died. I was holding her hand. Her parents had been with her for hours. They'd just stepped out to talk to the doctor. Suddenly, she started gasping for breath. I found out later that her lungs were filling with blood. She squeezed my hand and begged me not to let go. She begged me not to let her die. She was so afraid."

"You mustn't blame yourself. You didn't have the power to save her."

"No, but God could have."

"No one can know God's plan for each of us, Melissa."

"Maybe I didn't pray hard enough."

"None of what happened was your fault."

"I know that now, but when I was sixteen and Jenny died in front of me, the world stopped making sense. Nothing was right after that. I mean, what was the point of going to school if you might wake up one day and find out it's your last?"

"I'm sorry for your loss, Melissa, but blaming God instead of seeking His comfort won't help you heal."

The smile she managed was brittle. "I'm healed. Time heals all things. And I did it without God."

Chapter Nine

The next day was Saturday and Melissa spent the early-morning hours in her room. The sound of cartoons filled the house but she wasn't in the mood for animated antics. She still couldn't believe the things she had confided to Richard. He must think she was the most pathetic creature on the face of the earth.

As much as she hated to admit it, he was right about one thing. Talking seemed to help. She had had a dream about Jenny.

It wasn't the usual one, the one that had haunted her nights for so many years. This dream had been about their secret hiding place. In the dream, they were seven or eight years old. She and Jenny were huddled inside the hayloft of the abandoned carriage house at the back of Jenny's parents' property. They were giggling and playing house with the dolls they kept hidden there.

Melissa's doll was bundled in a tattered blanket and clutched lovingly in her arms as she walked around the perimeter of the old wooden floor pretending to be on her way to Jenny's home. She stopped and knocked on an imaginary door. Jenny leaped to her feet and answered the knock. "Oh, how lovely. You've brought your baby to see me."

The dream ended there, but when Melissa woke, a touch of warmth and happiness remained in her heart. It was nice to remember Jenny the way she was before she became ill.

A knock sounded on the real door to her current hiding place. An instant of trepidation made her hesitate, but she couldn't hide all day.

"Come in," she called.

Angela opened the door. "Are you up?"

From her seat in the chair by the window, Melissa answered, "Barely."

"Dave and I are off to work on the house. Do you have plans for today?"

"Nothing but a little laundry."

"The girls were asking if you could come with them to Aunt Lettie's this afternoon. Richard will take them, but he has some work he needs to do at his office. I hate to saddle Lettie with both girls for the afternoon without a little help. She isn't as young as she used to be and the girls can be…labor intensive at times."

"I'll be happy to visit with Lettie again. I really enjoyed meeting her the other night. She's quite a character."

"She is that. Thanks so much for doing this."

"What time are we leaving?"

"Not until after one o'clock. That should give you plenty of time to do your laundry." With a fluttering wave of her fingers, Angela left the room.

Melissa glanced at the clock on the wall. It was already nine. That might leave her enough time to do laundry, but it didn't leave her near enough time to decide what she would say to Richard when she saw him.

Should she act as though nothing happened? Did he think she was a nutcase? She certainly didn't want his pity. If he started acting as if he felt sorry for her, she would have to thump him upside the head. No, she would act as if nothing out of the ordinary had transpired.

Later, she couldn't decide if she was relieved or miffed that he acted as if she hadn't revealed to him the most painful experience of her life. Maybe he was used to women pouring out their sad sob stories. He was an attorney, after all. He must have heard a few confessions in his time.

His mood was jovial as he drove them to Lettie's home. He dropped Melissa, Lauren and Samantha off at the curb with barely a backward glance.

"Well, so much for pouring my heart out," Melissa muttered as his car rounded the corner and disappeared.

If he could act as though nothing had changed between them, so could she. The fact was, nothing *had* changed between them. It was only her foolish imagination that wanted to paint their relationship as more than it was.

Determined not to give him another thought, she followed the girls up the stairs where Lettie was waiting for them with a bright smile on her face.

Inside Lettie's cheerful, but antique-filled home, Melissa saw why Angela didn't want to leave the girls without supervision. The rambunctious pair could easily dispatch several thousand dollars' worth of china plates or porcelain figurines with little effort. Fortunately, Lettie had a way to keep them occupied and out of the living room.

"How would y'all like to bake something special with me?"

"Could we?" Lauren looked at Melissa with undisguised eagerness.

"If Miss Lettie says it's okay, I don't see why not."

"Cool," Samantha added, trying not to look as excited as her sister.

Lettie shooed them into the kitchen. "I've got to bake three apple pies for the church social tomorrow. If you girls help me, we'll have them done in no time."

She soon had Samantha and Melissa busy paring fresh apples while she showed Lauren how to measure flour and cut the shortening into the dough.

"Cut the flour into the shortening like this. You don't want to handle it too much."

"Why?" Lauren was peering into the bowl intently.

"It'll make the crust tough."

"Why?"

Lettie paused, then chuckled. "Child, I don't rightly know, but it does."

"Can I roll it out into a circle?" Lauren begged.

"You can roll the bottom and your sister can roll the top so both of you can say you made it."

When the first pie was finished and in the oven, Lettie gave both the girls the leftover dough. "My mother always let me make turnovers out of the extra. I called them teensy pies when I was little. You girls find some jam and make a few for me."

Samantha asked, "What kind should we make?"

"Surprise me," Lettie answered.

She left the girls working on the counter and sat at the table beside Melissa. Picking up her paring knife, she started in on the next pile of apples. "How is your father doing, Melissa?"

"Okay, I guess."

Lettie stopped peeling and peered at Melissa over the rim of her glasses. "You guess? Don't you know?"

Embarrassed to admit to this kindly woman that she hadn't been to see her dad, Melissa ducked her head. "Daddy and I haven't exactly been getting along."

"I see." Lettie began peeling again. After the fourth apple, her continued silence was more than Melissa could stand.

"I do plan to see him soon. Mother says he'll be home by Thanksgiving."

"That's good." Lettie kept paring. The quiet was broken only by the voices of the girls at the other end of the kitchen.

"It's not that I don't love my father," Melissa added to reassure Lettie and perhaps herself.

"Of course you do."

"I do. Only…"

"Only what?"

"He's going to be so disappointed in me," she finished in a small voice.

Reaching across the table, Lettie laid a hand over Melissa's. "Why on earth would he be disappointed in such a lovely young woman?"

Meeting Lettie's kind gaze, Melissa sighed. "Because I'm pregnant."

Lettie's eyebrows shot up. "Oh, I see. If you don't mind my asking, where is the baby's father?"

"Long gone. He doesn't want anything to do with us. Now you know why I can't face my father."

"That certainly makes it more difficult for you."

"Daddy will have a cow."

"Is your father a Christian man?"

"He goes to church."

"There's more to being a Christian than sitting in church, but it's a start. Have you thought that instead of 'having a cow' your father might order the fatted calf slain in celebration that his daughter has returned?"

Melissa gave her a look of disbelief. "No."

"Do you know the parable of the prodigal son?"

"Sort of."

Lettie left the room and came back a few minutes later with a Bible. She opened it and thumbed through a few pages until she found what she was looking for. "Melissa, I want you to listen to this story. In Luke 15, Jesus tells us the story of a man with two sons. The younger one said to his father, 'Father, give me my share of the estate.' So he divided his property between them.

"Not long after that, the younger son got together all he had, set off for a distant country and there squandered his wealth in wild living. After he had spent everything, there was a severe famine in that whole country, and he began to be in need. So he went and hired himself out to a citizen of that country, who sent him to his fields to feed pigs. He longed to fill his stomach with the pods that the pigs were eating, but no one gave him anything.

"When he came to his senses, he said, 'How many of my father's hired men have food to spare, and here I am starving to death! I will set out and go back to my father and say to him, Father, I have sinned against Heaven and against you. I am no longer worthy to be called your son. Make me like one of your hired men.' So he got up and went to his father.

"But while he was still a long way off, his father saw him and was filled with compassion for him. He ran to his son, threw his arms around him and kissed him.

"The son said to him, 'Father, I have sinned against Heaven and against you. I am no longer worthy to be called your son.'

"But the father said to his servants, 'Quick! Bring the best robe and put it on him. Put a ring on his finger and sandals on his feet. Bring the fattened calf and kill it. Let's have a feast and celebrate. For this son of mine was dead and is alive again, he was lost and is found.' So they began to celebrate.

"Meanwhile, the older son was in the field. When he came near the house, he heard music and dancing. So he called one of the servants and asked him what was going on. 'Your brother has come,' he replied, 'and your father has killed the fattened calf because he has him back safe and sound.'

"The older brother became angry and refused to go in. So his father went out and pleaded with him. But he answered his father, 'Look! All these years I've been slaving for you and never disobeyed your orders. Yet you never gave me even a young goat so I could celebrate with my friends. But when this son of yours who has squandered your property comes home, you kill the fattened calf for him!'

"'My son,' the father said, 'you are always with me, and everything I have is yours. But we had to celebrate and be glad, because this brother of yours was dead and is alive again, he was lost and is found.'"

Melissa listened intently to the old woman's voice. At the end of the story, Lettie closed the book and waited. Melissa said, "I'd love to think my father will welcome me with open arms, but I'm afraid I know him better than that."

"You'll never know for sure until you give him the chance. I can't imagine how it would hurt knowing my own child was so afraid of me that she couldn't come see me in the hospital."

"I want to see him, I do. Only…"

"Only what?"

"Only…this sounds so stupid."

"Child, you ain't said anything yet so it can't sound stupid."

"I'm afraid."

"Of your father's anger?"

"Yes, I'm afraid to face my dad, but I'm…I'm terrified of hospitals. Isn't that the stupidest thing you've ever heard?"

"I once heard a man say he had a horse that could drive a truck. Honestly, I think that was the stupidest thing I've ever heard. We can't always help being scared of things. Why, a spider will near send me into a fit, and you and me both know I'm bigger than a bitsy old spider. Why do you think you're scared of hospitals?"

"After my friend Jenny died, I couldn't set foot inside one without shaking like a leaf."

"Do tell? When did your friend die?"

"Just before Christmas, when we were sixteen. It's odd. I haven't talked to anyone about Jenny since her funeral…until yesterday."

"What happened yesterday?"

"Richard asked me about her. He said it would help to talk about things that trouble me. I've always heard that, but I never really believed it until now."

"Are you still angry with her?"

Puzzled, Melissa said, "With who?"

"With your friend, for dying."

Melissa opened her mouth to deny it, but the words stuck in her throat. How could she be mad at Jenny? Jenny hadn't asked to die. Shaking her head, she said, "That's ridiculous."

"I was mad at my Gilbert for a long time after he passed away. I was mad at God, too."

"Isn't that against your faith?"

"The good Lord has broad shoulders. He took all my anger and sorrow into Himself. In the end, I was healed by His love and by the love Gilbert and I shared. We had a good life, but it's nothing compared to the eternal glory waiting for me. Every morning when I wake up, I'm a little sad because the Lord didn't call me home. I'm eighty-eight, you know. But each day I recall my Gilbert's voice saying, 'What you got planned today, Lettie Mae?' just like he used to ask me, and I know it's the Lord's way of telling me my work on earth ain't done. He's got a plan for me even if I can't see it."

"You mean you aren't afraid of dying?"

"'Course I am! I'm human, aren't I? It's natural to fear dying, but Jesus went down into the grave and rose from the dead to show us that our fears and doubts are but a veil that keeps us from seeing clearly the glory awaiting us. When my time comes, and it will, it comes to everyone, I believe Jesus will pull the veil from my eyes and I'll see all those I love waiting to greet me."

"It's nice to think I could see Jenny again."

"Those that die in the Lord are never lost. You should talk to her."

"Talk to her? You mean, go to her grave?"

"It helps some folks to visit their loved ones that have passed on. I always feel close to Gilbert when I'm there. I go to visit regular like."

Their conversation was interrupted when Lauren raced to the table. "Aunt Lettie, we finished our teensy pies. I made peach ones and Samantha made strawberry."

"That's wonderful. We'll bake them up as soon as the one in the oven is finished. I reckon Melissa and I have enough apples peeled for two more pies. Melissa, why don't you come into the living room? I have something you might like to see."

Melissa followed her into the next room and waited as Lettie opened one of the curved doors on an antique cherrywood credenza and withdrew a box filled with yellowed newspaper clippings. "I got these out after meeting you the other night. Did I mention that I knew your grandfather Hamilton?"

"No. How did you know Grandpa?"

"I was a reporter for his paper in 1936. These are a few of my articles."

Melissa took the box and sat on the plush red velvet of the camel-back sofa. She began to leaf through the pile, reading snippets of news about Davis Landing before World War II.

"Lettie, these are wonderful. I remember my grandmother talking about this fire and how she saw the orange light in the sky all night long and wondered if the *Dispatch* building would still be standing in the morning. Only the bylines on these say Leonard Corbet."

"That was my pen name. It would have been scandalous to use my own name."

"Why?"

"Honey, a nice Southern girl didn't work as a reporter for the newspaper in those days. My folks would have had a fit if they knew. They thought I was a secretary, which I was for the most part. But I loved going out to cover the news. Your grandpa, he always said a woman could do the job as well as a man, but not many men felt that way back then."

"So you never received credit for your work?"

"No, but I got my paycheck, and that was enough in those days. Times were hard. The country was in the depths of the Depression. My name in a byline wasn't as important as the little bit of money I earned. Besides, there were other women doing the same thing."

An idea began to form in the back of Melissa's mind. What if she could get the paper to do a story about women like Lettie?

"Do you know their names?"

"I reckon I can find a few in my old letters in the attic. Why?"

A knock sounded at the door and both Lauren and Samantha hurried to answer it. Beating her big sister by a narrow margin, Lauren pulled open the door. "Oh, it's you," she said, clearly dejected.

"If that's the kind of welcome I get, maybe I should leave."

At the sound of Richard's amused voice, Melissa's

pulse accelerated. She hadn't realized how much she had been missing him and how eager she was to spend time with him. She only hoped her eagerness wasn't apparent to the others.

"Sorry, Uncle Richard," Lauren apologized. "It's just that we don't want to go home yet. Our teensy pies aren't done."

"Come in, dear," Lettie called. "I'm just bending Melissa's ear about the good old days."

Richard walked in and took a seat on the sofa beside Melissa. "Your stories are always worth listening to, Aunt Lettie. Even the ones I've heard a hundred times. We'll stay until you're done baking, girls."

The timer on the oven began buzzing. Lettie rose and handed the box to Melissa. "Come on girls, my pie is done. It's time to put yours in. Don't forget to put your initials in the crust with a fork so you can tell which is which."

The girls hurried into the kitchen ahead of their aunt. Richard leaned close to Melissa and whispered, "What are teensy pies?"

The scent of his aftershave engulfed her and his breathy whisper tickled her ear. It took all her powers of concentration to reply in a normal tone of voice. "They're popovers made with leftover pie dough."

"Why don't they call them popovers?"

"Where's the fun in that?"

"Must be a girl thing."

He didn't move away. She hoped she wasn't blushing. She liked it far too much when he was close.

"What do you have here?" He picked up one of the yellowed strips of newspaper.

"Your aunt was telling me about her years as a reporter for my grandfather's paper."

"Lettie was a reporter? I didn't know that."

"Not many people knew. Apparently it was quite scandalous behavior for a young, unmarried woman in those days. I wonder how many other women of Lettie's generation were denied credit for their work for the same reason?"

"I'm sure there must have been a few, but after all this time, it would be hard to find out who they were."

"It's not fair. Lettie and the others should be recognized for what they accomplished."

"What can you do about it now?"

She grinned at him. "Are you kidding? My family owns the paper. I'll need to do some research, but I think I can convince Ed Bradshaw that this is a story worth writing. In fact, I know someone who might jump at the chance to write it." She thought of Felicity and how she had spoken of her struggles in a male-dominated profession.

"Do you really think so?"

"Yes, something tells me this would make a great personal interest story for the paper or maybe even for our magazine. I'd really like to find out more about these women. I think it's time to give credit where credit is due, or in this case, long overdue."

Richard couldn't help but notice the way Melissa's eyes sparkled with excitement. It was obvious that she wanted to pursue this project. He was glad. She needed something of her own to sink her teeth into. She needed something besides her own problems to focus on.

"What can I do to help?" he asked.

"I'm not sure, but I'll let you know." Her smile was so bright and her enthusiasm so genuine that he wanted to kiss her. He leaned closer.

An Important Message from the Editors of Steeple Hill Books

Dear Reader,

Because you've chosen to read one of our fine romance novels, we'd like to say "thank you!" And, as a **special** way to thank you, we've selected <u>two more</u> of the books you love so much, **and** a surprise gift to send you — absolutely <u>FREE!</u>

Please enjoy them with our compliments...

Jean Gordon

Editor,
Love Inspired®

FREE GIFT
EDITOR'S SEAL
THANK YOU

Peel off seal and place inside...

HOW TO VALIDATE YOUR
EDITOR'S FREE GIFT!
"THANK YOU"

1 Peel off the FREE GIFTS SEAL from front cover. Place it in the space provided at right. This automatically entitles you to receive two free books and an exciting surprise gift.

2 Send back this card and you'll get 2 Love Inspired® books. These books have a combined cover price of $9.98 in the U.S. and $11.98 in Canada, but they are yours to keep absolutely FREE!

3 There's no catch. You're under no obligation to buy anything. We charge nothing—ZERO—for your first shipment. And you don't have to make any minimum number of purchases—not even one!

4 We call this line Love Inspired because each month you'll receive books that are filled with joy, faith and traditional values. The stories will lift your spirits and gladden your heart! You'll like the convenience of getting them delivered to your home well before they are in stores. And you'll love our discount prices, too!

5 We hope that after receiving your free books you'll want to remain a subscriber. But the choice is yours—to continue or cancel, anytime at all! So why not take us up on our invitation, with no risk of any kind. You'll be glad you did!

6 And remember. . . just for validating your Editor's Free Gift Offer, we'll send you 2 books and a gift, *ABSOLUTELY FREE!*

YOURS FREE!
We'll send you a fabulous surprise gift absolutely FREE, simply for accepting our no-risk offer!

® and ™ are trademarks owned and used by the trademark owner and/or its licensee.

Order online at:
www.LoveInspiredBooks.com

- Two inspirational romance books
- An exciting surprise gift

▼ DETACH AND MAIL CARD TODAY!! ▼

YES!

PLACE FREE GIFTS SEAL HERE

I have placed my Editor's "thank you" Free Gifts seal in the space provided above. Please send me the 2 FREE books and gift for which I qualify. I understand that I am under no obligation to purchase anything further, as explained on the opposite page.

313 IDL EE36   **113 IDL EE4J**

FIRST NAME	LAST NAME

ADDRESS

APT.#	CITY

STATE/PROV.	ZIP/POSTAL CODE

Thank You!

(LI-EC-06) © 1997 STEEPLE HILL BOOKS

Offer limited to one per household and not valid to current Love Inspired® subscribers. All orders subject to approval. Credit or debit balances in a customer's account(s) may be offset by any other outstanding balance owed by or to the customer. Please allow 4 to 6 weeks for delivery.

Steeple Hill Reader Service™— Here's How It Works:

Accepting your 2 free books and gift places you under no obligation to buy anything. You may keep the books and gift and return the shipping statement marked "cancel." If you do not cancel, about a month later we will send you 4 additional books and bill you just $3.99 each in the U.S., or $4.74 each in Canada, plus 25¢ shipping & handling per book and applicable taxes if any.* That's the complete price, and — compared to cover prices of $4.99 each in the U.S. and $5.99 each in Canada — it's quite a bargain! You may cancel at any time, but if you choose to continue, every month we'll send you 4 more books, which you may either purchase at the discount price...or return to us and cancel your subscription.

*Terms and prices subject to change without notice. Sales tax applicable in N.Y.
Canadian residents will be charged applicable provincial taxes and GST.

If offer card is missing write to: Steeple Hill Reader Service, 3010 Walden Ave., P.O. Box 1867, Buffalo, NY 14240-1867

BUSINESS REPLY MAIL
FIRST-CLASS MAIL   PERMIT NO. 717-003   BUFFALO, NY

POSTAGE WILL BE PAID BY ADDRESSEE

STEEPLE HILL READER SERVICE
3010 WALDEN AVE
PO BOX 1867
BUFFALO NY 14240-9952

NO POSTAGE
NECESSARY
IF MAILED
IN THE
UNITED STATES

Chapter Ten

Richard bent toward Melissa, but just then, Lettie and the girls returned from the kitchen. He sat back and pretended interest in the shoe box contents. At least the interruption had come before he'd made a fool of himself and embarrassed them both.

Melissa turned her attention to his aunt. "Lettie, what would you think of my paper doing a story about your reporting back in the day?"

"Are you pulling my leg?"

"Not at all. I'm serious about looking into this story."

Lettie grinned. "I reckon it won't hurt my reputation after all these years, but I'm not sure it's newsworthy."

"Our paper is always looking for personal interest pieces. If you wouldn't mind, I'd like to do a little more research on your work and the work of any other women you can recall."

"All right, you come over tomorrow afternoon and I'll have some letters and such for you to look at."

"That would be great."

After spending another hour with Lettie, Richard

drove Lauren, Samantha and Melissa home. He followed them into the house, but as the girls headed for the kitchen to store their teensy pies, he stopped Melissa with a hand on her arm.

"I have the adoption forms and information for you. They came in the mail to my office today."

"Your friend didn't waste any time." She turned away but not before he saw the troubled frown that chased the happiness from her face.

Lord, lend this woman Your strength. Help her make the right decision.

"Melissa, if you aren't ready for this, I understand."

Her chin came up as she faced him again. "I'm ready."

After setting his briefcase on the coffee table, he opened it and withdrew a bundle of papers. "I'll let you look these over. I'll be around if you have any questions."

She nodded but didn't answer as she took the forms and walked down the hall toward her room.

"Melissa, wait."

She stopped and looked back over her shoulder. He shoved his hands in his pockets. "I wanted to invite you to attend church with us in the morning."

"Thanks, but I'll pass."

He walked toward her, uncertain of his next words. God's infinite love was waiting for her if only she would open her heart, but how could he make her believe that? He stopped beside her and asked gently, "Why?"

She looked down. "I'd just rather not."

"Are you ashamed to be seen in church?"

"Maybe."

"You don't have anything to be ashamed of."

"Oh, some people would disagree."

"Tell me something. Are you sorry for the way you behaved?"

She folded her arms across her chest. "That's a stupid question. Of course I am. I know that I hurt other people. If I could undo the choices I've made, I would, but life doesn't have a rewind button, so I'm stuck with my regrets."

"Have you forgiven Dean?"

"I don't know. Maybe. I used him to get back at my father. I guess I shouldn't be angry that he used me, too."

"All God asks of us is to forgive those that trespass against us and to seek His forgiveness for our sins. Jesus did the hard part. He died for us."

"I don't want to be a hypocrite. And that's exactly what I would be if I stepped inside a church. Besides, there's so much sadness and pain in the world. Why should God bother with my petty troubles?"

"Your troubles aren't petty and your needs aren't a burden to God. He has the capacity to know and love each and every human on earth. You are as special to him as Samantha and Lauren, as special as Lettie or myself. All the stars in the sky are there by His command. Even the birds in the air are held up by His will. He has no limits. If you truly want to change, you can. He will help you every step of the way."

"He turned His back on me and on Jenny."

"I've heard you say that before. I'm pretty good at reading people, Melissa. It's kind of a gift I have. And that gift is telling me that you're lying. You don't believe God abandoned you. You were angry. You wanted to punish someone for Jenny's death and the only one you could find was God."

"You're right. I hate Him for taking Jenny away."

"I know you do, but your anger hasn't punished God, Melissa. The only one hurting…is you."

She looked at him, her eyes filled with turmoil and icy bitterness. "Are you finished now?"

He nodded, feeling as if he had lost the most important argument of his life.

Melissa fled down the hall to her room and away from Richard and the confusion he brought to her. Why couldn't he and his family leave her alone? If she didn't want to attend church, if she didn't want to love God, that was her business. She closed the door and leaned her head against the wood. A tear slid from the corner of her eye and she wiped at it with the back of her hand. The crackle of paper drew her attention to the pages she had clenched in her fist.

She moved away from the door and sat on the bed, then carefully spread them out around her. This was the official start to the adoption—her means of solving her unwanted problem. Only, why did it become harder every day to think about giving up her baby? She had to. How else could she right the mistakes she had made? Getting her life back together was tough enough. There was no way she could do that and raise a child…was there?

Maybe this was her punishment for her sins.

No, she wouldn't think that way. This was her decision and hers alone. God had nothing to do with it. She was doing this because it was the best thing for her—and for the baby.

She picked up the first paper. It was a Dear Birth Mother letter written by a couple from Memphis. That wasn't too far away.

Dear Birth Mother,

I know that we are strangers to you. That very fact makes it difficult to find the words to convey how much we will love your baby if you give us the chance. We offer your child a financially secure life filled with happiness. What more can we say? We are asking for the greatest gift you can bestow. Please consider us.

Melissa laid the letter down as tears pricked her eyes. She hadn't expected the message it to be so heartfelt. The woman was begging for a child to love. Picking up another sheet of paper, she saw it contained questions a birth mother should ask herself before making an adoption plan. She read them carefully.

Why are you placing your child for adoption?

Will you be able to explain it to the child someday?

How does the child's father feel about this plan?

Do you want the adoptive parents to be birthing coaches?

Would you allow them to be in the delivery room?

Would you like to spend time alone with the baby in the hospital?

Do you have a name for the baby?

Would you like to receive letters and pictures over time?

Would you like phone contact with the adoptive family?

Do you want to see the child occasionally? How often?

Will anyone else in your family want this privilege?

Is there anyone you would specifically want to exclude?

Melissa dropped the paper. Suddenly, it was all too real. It was too much. How could she possibly make decisions that would affect so many lives? Did Dean care if she put their baby up for adoption? Would her parents and siblings want to visit and see pictures? Did she want strangers in the delivery room with her? What if these people gave the baby a ridiculous name?

She rose and went to stand at the window. She pulled the drapes aside, but she didn't really see the grass or the trees blazing with color in the late-afternoon light. She placed her hand on her stomach.

"Why should it matter what name someone who wants you chooses?" she whispered. "Any name is better than 'my little problem.' That's the only thing I've called you. I didn't want to name you. I thought that I wouldn't become as attached to you if you didn't have a name. How silly is that?

"I can't run away from this, can I? No matter what I do, you'll be with me every step of the way."

Melissa let the curtains fall into place and turned back to the bed. With a heavy heart, she picked up the letters and began to read them one by one and sort them into piles of yes, maybe and no. She wiped tears away more than once before she was done. Each letter added to the no pile meant another hopeful couple would keep on waiting for a child. Afterward, she found a pencil and a sheet of paper and began to answer the questions on the form.

Nearly an hour had gone by before she heard a knock at her door. She looked up and said, "Come in."

Samantha peeked in. "Are you busy?"

Melissa gathered her papers together. "I'm just finishing. What can I do for you?"

"Would you have time to help me practice my vocal scales?"

"Of course." She reached over and put her papers in the drawer of the bedside table.

"Cool." Samantha entered carrying her keyboard under one arm. "I want to blow them away with my singing tomorrow at church."

"I'm sure you will."

Lauren came in behind Samantha and joined them on the bed. Sprawling on her stomach, Lauren propped her chin on her hands and watched her sister set up the keyboard. Samantha glared at her. "Don't you have something to do?"

Lauren smiled and said, "Nope."

"Find something."

"I don't mind if she stays," Melissa said, pulling the keyboard onto her lap.

"Uncle Richard said you won't be coming to church with us in the morning. I wish you would." Samantha's statement took Melissa by surprise.

Heaving a weary sigh, she shook her head. "I'm not a churchgoer."

"Sweet," Lauren said. "That means I can stay home with you."

Melissa half turned to see the child better. "What?"

"I'm tired of going to church every Sunday. I want to sleep in and goof off. Who needs church, anyway?"

Samantha rolled her eyes. "Oh, right. Like Mom and Dad are going to let you do that."

"If Melissa doesn't have to go to church, neither do I."

"Whoa!" Melissa said. "I'm an adult. You are not. You have to do what your parents tell you. Don't put me in the middle of this."

"That's right, Lauren. You're just a kid," Samantha chided.

"I won't always be a kid. Someday I'll be a newspaper reporter, and travel, and have a cool life like hers. Maybe I'll have a boyfriend in a band. Maybe I'll even be in a band myself."

The blatant hero worship in Lauren's words stunned Melissa. While she didn't need God in her life, the idea that she might have influenced this child to turn away from Him shocked her. The revelation triggered a flood of confusing thoughts. She never expected to be a role model. Her anger at God was personal, but until now, she hadn't considered the kind of example she was setting. Richard and his sister were probably sorry they had offered her a place to stay.

"Lauren, you mustn't think you want to be like me. I don't want you to give up going to church because I don't go."

"Why?"

"Because…I don't know…because my life has been shallow and pointless up until now. I've hurt people who love me. You don't want a life like mine. Trust me." She reached out and laid a hand on Lauren's shoulder.

Lauren's disappointment was painfully clear. "You

think I'm just a dumb kid who doesn't know what she wants."

"I think *I* was a dumb kid who didn't know what she wanted. I don't want to see anyone make the same mistakes I did."

She glanced toward the papers on the bedside table. "Sometimes the price we have to pay for those mistakes is way too high."

Sunday morning Richard's entire family went to church and Melissa stayed behind. Her intention was to catch up on some reading, but instead she found herself wandering from one incredibly quiet room to the next until she found herself in Richard's study.

She trailed her fingers across the edge of his oversize desk as she walked around it. Sitting in his chair only made her feel small, not large and powerful the way he seemed when he was seated in it. The photos on the desk were mostly of his family: Angela, Dave and the girls at the beach; Lettie, looking happy and proud beside a man with thick, gray hair slicked back and a handlebar mustache waxed into points.

One of the photos she picked up to examine more closely. It was Richard when he was younger, perhaps in high school. He was standing on the steps of a small white house. Beside him sat a collie looking up with adoring eyes.

She returned the picture to its place and picked up the last one. It was of Richard and her father the year they won the charity golf classic, a fund-raiser for the new hospital. They looked happy and relaxed, each of them holding up one side of a silver trophy. Her father was fortunate to have a friend like Richard. She was fortunate to have him for a friend, too. She spent a long time looking at her father and trying to remember the last time she had made him smile.

She set the photo down and dipped her hands in the jelly bean jar. She scrounged around until she found several cherry ones and popped them in her mouth.

Rising, she crossed the floor to the bookcases and studied the titles. For the most part, they were law books, thick and imposing and offering little temptation to browse through their pages. At the end of one shelf she found a group of westerns, a half-dozen mysteries and a well-worn bible. She lifted it down and opened it to the page marked with a thin gold ribbon. It was Proverbs.

She read part of the passage aloud. "'My son, if you accept my words and store up my commands within you, turning your ear to wisdom and applying your heart to understanding, and if you call out for insight and cry aloud for understanding, and if you look for it as for silver and search for it as for hidden treasure, then you will understand the fear of the Lord and the knowledge of God.'"

Why had he marked this section? Did he seek wisdom and understanding? With the exception of her mother, Melissa considered Richard to be one of the wisest and most understanding people she knew. Was this where he found his patience and kindness? Thoughtfully, she closed the book and returned it to the shelf.

Later that afternoon, Melissa was once again seated in Lettie's front room. The elderly woman had three large, leather-bound scrapbooks and several worn shoe boxes set out on the dining room table.

"These are all I could find. I hope it's what you need," Lettie said.

Melissa opened the first book. Black-and-white photos and newspaper clippings with crumbling edges were affixed to the thick pages with brittle tape. In a shoe box, she found dozens of letters, their ink faded by time. For the next hour, she pored over the letters with interest, taking notes on dates and names. All in all, she discovered four other women who mentioned articles they had written.

"Are you finding what you wanted?" Lettie asked.

Melissa folded the last letter and returned it to the box. "I am. Now I need to go through the archives at the paper. If I can match some of these articles, I can see from the bylines the names the women used. Are any of these ladies still living?"

"Only Belle Crawford. She is up at the nursing home in Langford, but I haven't seen her in over a year. I believe her son owns a pharmacy over there. You might check with him."

Melissa wrote down the information. When she looked up, she saw Lettie had put on her coat and was setting a ruched, black velvet hat into place on her head. Feeling guilty for monopolizing the generous woman's time, Melissa stood and stuffed her notes into her bag. "I'm sorry. You should have told me I was keeping you from something."

"You weren't, sugar. In fact, I was hoping you might come with me. I'm not feeling all that spry today."

"Are you sure you should be going out if you aren't feeling well?"

Lettie pulled on a pair of black gloves. "I haven't

missed a Sunday afternoon with my Gilbert in twenty-seven years. I'm not going to miss today because I'm feeling a mite peaked. If you don't mind coming with me, that is?"

"Of course I don't mind coming with you."

Lettie walked over and took Melissa's face between her hands. "You're such a sweet child to indulge an old woman you barely know."

"You're sweet to indulge my interest in these women's stories. I can't thank you enough for all this information."

"It's good to have a passion for something. I like that you want to give credit to others. Now, let's get going before it gets dark. You can drive, can't you?"

"Of course."

"My car is in the garage around back."

Twenty minutes later, Melissa turned Lettie's gray Pontiac into the entrance of the cemetery on the outskirts of Davis Landing. The wrought-iron gates stood open, and as she passed under the archway, Melissa realized that she hadn't been here since Jenny's funeral.

It had rained that day—hard pouring rain that seemed to beat the mourners into smaller versions of themselves. Everyone had huddled under umbrellas. She remembered her father, his head uncovered, holding his umbrella over Jenny's parents as they supported each other from the car to the striped awning set up over the grave. She remembered the flowers, their delicate petals knocked loose by the deluge as Jenny's coffin was carried from the hearse. It had been a terrible day.

The road into the cemetery forked just beyond the entrance. Lettie pointed to the right. "Gilbert is up by the statue of Jesus and the lambs. I'll tell you when to stop."

Melissa nodded and started in that direction. She pulled over at a word from Lettie and turned off the engine. Lettie opened the door, but paused and looked over her shoulder. "Would you mind terribly if I asked you not to come up with me? I'd rather be alone."

"I don't mind waiting."

"You should go and see your friend while you are here."

Melissa looked down the road ahead. If she remembered correctly, Jenny's grave was past the next group of loblolly pines. Shaking her head, she said, "No, I'll wait here for you in case you get to feeling worse."

"Worse than what? Oh, yes. Well, the truth is I'm feeling much, much better. It must be the fresh air."

Melissa frowned at her companion. "Miss Lettie, did you fib to me?"

Lettie opened her mouth and closed it again, then managed a sheepish grin. "I wouldn't call it so much a fib, as a plan."

"A plan for what?"

"To get you to come here and see your friend, Jenny." She got out of the car and leaned down to look in. "You have a lot to tell her. Go on."

Lettie closed the door and began walking across the immaculately manicured lawns to a small bench beside one of the lambs clustered at Christ's feet. She opened her purse and drew out a small white rosebud. After laying it on the brown granite tombstone in front of her, she sat down and bowed her head.

Melissa stepped out of the car and stared down the gravel road toward the pines. It looked like a short walk, but it was one that had taken her seven years to make.

The crushed white rock crunched under her shoes as

she began walking. The world was so quiet. All she heard besides her own footsteps was the sound of the breeze in the pines as she passed them. Their marvelous smell scented the air with a fragrance that was pure and crisp. Around her, the grounds sloped toward the river in gentle undulating rolls marked by carved stones in all shapes and sizes.

The stand of pines separated a newer part of the cemetery from the old. This part lacked the large and ornate headstones of the older sections, but the identical low markers gave the hillside a solemn dignity. It took her a few more minutes to find Jenny's stone.

Kneeling down, Melissa brushed a few grass clippings from the top of the marker. Quietly, she read the inscription.

"Jennifer LeAnn Wilson, Our blessed daughter sleeps not here, but lives in Heaven above."

"Oh, Jenny, I hope that's true. I hope you aren't here, but someplace wonderful, someplace filled with love and happiness. Richard believes that, and so does Lettie, and my mother, and so many other people that I respect. I want to believe, too."

Settling back on her heels, Melissa stared at the date of Jenny's death. It was a date etched in her mind as firmly as it was etched in the stone before her.

"I'm sorry, Jenny. I'm sorry I couldn't hold on to you hard enough to keep you from dying. I'm sorry I didn't run and get help or your parents. I know it broke your mother's heart that she wasn't with you. I hope you can forgive me for that."

Melissa sniffed and wiped her nose. "Look at me, I'm crying again. That's just about all I get done anymore.

My hormones are way out of whack. Did you know that I'm pregnant? Remember how we used to play with our dolls and pretend we were off to visit each other while our husbands were working?

"I'm pregnant, but I really messed up the husband part. I wanted to love Dean. I thought I did, but I got that wrong, too. Now, I'm trying not to mess up this poor kid's life, as well.

"Oh, Jenny, why did you have to die? Why couldn't you have stayed here and talked me out of all the stupid things I've done since you've been gone? I depended on you."

Melissa pressed the heels of her hands into her eyes to stem the tears that threatened. When she had gained a measure of control, she reached down and began pulling up little tufts of grass.

"Here I am, still trying to blame someone else for my mistakes. I know you didn't want to die. I guess I even know that I couldn't have prevented it.

"It's funny, but all this time I didn't realize how mad I was at you for leaving me until Lettie said that she had been mad at her husband for dying. Maybe I'm not such an oddball after all."

For a long time, Melissa sat quietly in the grass, her legs folded beneath her as she thought about Jenny and the fun times they had shared as children and as carefree teenagers. The happy memories soon outnumbered the sad ones.

A small brown thrush flew down from the pines and landed on a marker only a few feet away. For a moment, it watched Melissa with bright eyes, turning its head left and right. It warbled a few bright notes, then it took flight and sailed toward the river.

As she watched it soar away, Melissa noticed that her heart was feeling lighter. She rose and dusted off her jeans. "Thanks for listening, Jenny, and thanks for being such a great friend. I love you, and I'll never forget you. And I won't stay away so long next time. I promise."

When she turned around, Melissa saw Lettie waiting for her down at the edge of the road. Without a word, Melissa joined her. Arm in arm, they walked back to the car.

Chapter Eleven

At work the next morning, Melissa looked up to see Richard standing beside her cubicle. "What are you doing here?" she asked in surprise.

He glanced at his watch. "You have a doctor's appointment in half an hour. I'm here to give you a ride."

She knew about the appointment. It was simply another step toward ending her little problem.

No, don't think of it that way. Think of it as making sure you can give someone a healthy child.

"The clinic isn't that far. I can walk."

"I'm sure you can, but I'm already here. I hate to think I took off work for nothing."

Melissa gathered her purse and jacket from the back of her chair. "Will some mob boss go free because you aren't in the courtroom?"

"Hardly."

"In that case, I accept your offer of a ride."

Fifteen minutes later they stood in the waiting room at Dr. Kathy Miller's office. The room was small and cozy, with cheerful walls decorated with primary colors and oversize crayon cutouts. In one corner stood an enclosed play area for children. Only one other young woman sat on the blue plastic chairs. Melissa nodded as she took a seat across from her. Richard sat beside Melissa, looking as if he felt decidedly out of place.

She leaned toward him. "You don't have to wait. I can walk or get a cab when I'm done."

"I don't mind waiting." He picked up a copy of her family's *Nashville Living* magazine from the low, rectangular coffee table in front of them.

She gave him a grateful smile. "Thanks for keeping me company. I know it isn't rational, but medical places really do give me the creeps."

He gave her a sympathetic smile. "I thought that might be the case."

"When are you due?" The woman seated across the small waiting room pointed to Melissa's stomach.

"The end of February," Melissa replied.

"No fooling? Me, too. You sure aren't showing much. I'm already as big as a house. I keep telling the doctor it must be twins but she says there's only one. Have you got names picked out? The sonogram says mine is a boy. We're thinking about calling him Colin Leroy. What do you think of that?"

"It's a nice name."

A middle-aged nurse in sea-green scrubs entered the room from the hallway that led back to the exam rooms. "Mrs. Marks, the doctor will see you now."

Melissa watched in relief as the woman exited the room. Her plans were so much different than those of the happy young mother. How could she bring into a conversation about due dates and baby names the fact that she planned to give her child up for adoption?

Ten minutes later, the nurse was back for Melissa. As she rose to follow the nurse, the door opened and two more expectant women walked in. The doctor's practice was obviously a busy one. It was with some trepidation that Melissa followed the nurse to the exam room. If only she had asked her mother or one of her sisters to come with her, she wouldn't have to do this alone.

Inside the room, a short woman with curly black hair sat on a chrome stool beside the exam table. Dressed in a white lab coat over green scrubs, she was intently scribbling notes in a folder. When she was done, she closed the file, exchanging it for Melissa's. Rising, she held out her hand. "Hello, I'm Dr. Miller."

Melissa took the offered hand and forced a smile. "I'm happy to meet you."

She wasn't. Already she could feel her fears sprouting in a crawling sensation on the back of her neck.

"Please, have a seat." The doctor indicated the black vinyl bed. "I understand this is your first visit to us."

Melissa met her gaze, intent on maintaining control of her emotions. "Yes, I saw a doctor in Detroit when I first learned I was pregnant, but I haven't seen anyone since."

The doctor took her seat on the stool and rolled close. "Prenatal care is very important for the health of both mother and baby. I hope you'll continue seeing me. The nurse will check your temperature and other vital signs. Undress and put on this gown and I'll be back in a few minutes."

The exam lasted close to twenty minutes. Melissa answered all the nurse's questions and tried to ignore the

claustrophobic size of the room and the smell of anti-
septics that reminded her vividly of Jenny's last days.

*Relax. Breathe. This is almost over. Richard is close
by. He's just beyond that door in the waiting room. You
don't want him to see you running out of the building
like a madwoman, do you?*

The snap of the doctor's latex gloves when she pulled
them off made Melissa flinch. "Everything looks good,
except your blood pressure is a little high. I'll want to
keep an eye on that. All we need now is a sonogram to
check out junior."

Melissa swallowed hard. "How long will that take?"

"I'm a little backed up today. Hopefully, not more
than half an hour."

Another thirty minutes in this room? Melissa didn't
think she could do it. She pulled the sheet up to her chin.
"Could Richard wait with me?"

"Certainly. I'll have him step in."

"Thank you." Gripping the sheet, she closed her eyes
and began to count. Anything to keep from thinking.

She was up to fifty-five before the door opened. The
nurse came in followed by Richard. His eyes were filled
with concern. His frown etched a crease between his
brows. "What's wrong? Is it the baby?"

"No, the baby's fine. I'm…I'm just—" She glanced
at the nurse, unable to go on in front of a stranger.

He moved forward and took her hand. She gripped
it tightly. Without letting go, he bent down and pulled
the stool over, then sat close beside her. When the
nurse started to leave, he said, "Can you leave the door
open, please?"

She did as he asked and he turned back to Melissa

with a smile. "Did I tell you what Lauren did after church yesterday? It was the cutest thing."

She focused on his face, grateful for his presence. With the door open the room didn't feel so close. "What did she do?"

"It was partly my fault. We stayed after church for the box social and I mentioned that if we didn't hurry, we wouldn't get a piece of Lettie's pie. She's quite famous for them. I didn't even notice that Lauren was gone until Angela said something. We found Lauren and her friend Talia standing in front of the dessert table directing traffic around them. They had one of Lettie's pies hidden under the table."

"At least you got a piece."

"The thing was, several of the boys from their class had seen the move. By the time Lauren raised the tablecloth to show me where she'd hidden the pie, there were only crumbs left in the pan and three very guilty-looking, stuffed boys sitting beside the pan."

"You probably shouldn't have pie, anyway. Too many calories."

"Are you the diet police, now?"

"I am. Call me Sergeant Pepperoni of the nutrition patrol."

He grabbed his chest and closed his eyes as if in pain. "Oh, don't talk about pizza. I haven't had a slice in months."

She grinned at his performance. Little by little her fear had faded while he was talking.

By the time the doctor rolled in the sonogram machine, she was feeling well enough to let go of Richard's hand.

He stood and shoved his hands in his pockets. "I'll be right outside."

The doctor said, "You don't have to run off, Daddy. Stay and get a peek at your baby."

Melissa knew she was blushing to the roots of her hair because her face felt as hot as a pizza oven. She glanced at Richard. He was blushing, too. She wished suddenly that he *was* her child's father. He would make a wonderful daddy.

He said, "I'm sorry, Doctor, but there is some misunderstanding. I'm not the father."

"Oh, I'm sorry." She looked a bit flustered.

"Can he stay, anyway?" Melissa begged. "He's a friend."

The doctor nodded. "I don't see why not. Take a seat. This won't take long." She carefully folded down the sheet and folded up the gown, preserving Melissa's modesty until only the small mound of her tummy was exposed. After positioning the machine, she applied a clear gel to the wand she held and placed it on Melissa.

At once, Melissa heard a crackle of static, then a rapid thump, thump, thump. "What's that?"

"It's your baby's heartbeat." The doctor didn't look up as she adjusted knobs on the keyboard.

"That's my baby's heartbeat? Wow."

Melissa glanced at Richard. He had a bemused look on his face.

"It's kind of fast, isn't it?" he asked.

"Actually, it's right on target. I'm just going to take a look around."

She moved the wand over Melissa's stomach, pausing to add more gel every once in a while. Melissa found herself holding Richard's hand again. She wasn't quite sure if she had reached for him or if he had reached for her. It didn't matter. She drew comfort from his touch. How would she ever be able to thank him for staying with her?

After what seemed like an eternity, Dr. Miller spoke again. "Okay, I'm done here. Would you like to know if you are having a boy or a girl?"

Melissa's heart lurched. "I'm not sure."

Did she want to know? Would it make it easier to choose a family or would it make it harder? She looked at Richard. He shrugged, but she could see the interest in his face.

"I guess I'd like to know," she said at last.

"You are having a girl."

The doctor turned the machine so Melissa could see the screen. A gray cone of light outlined a small alien with a big head, a round tummy and impossibly long legs flexed beneath her floating in a dark world. As she watched, the baby moved one hand to her face.

Melissa looked at the doctor in astonishment. "Is she sucking her thumb?"

"She is."

"Wow." The word didn't even begin to describe the awe running rampant though her. A girl. She was having a baby girl. A girl would need a pink, frilly dress and one of those cute headbands with a bow on it. This unexpected, undesired, thumping lump in her belly was a baby girl who could stretch and suck her thumb. A burst of love, painful in its intensity, poured out of Melissa's heart. This wasn't an unfortunate problem. This was her daughter. Suddenly one tiny foot shot upward and the screen wavered as static crackled loudly.

Dr. Miller laughed. "It looks like she prefers her privacy. She just kicked my wand."

With a flip of a switch, the doctor turned the machine off. Melissa opened her mouth to protest, but closed it quickly. She wanted to see more of her baby girl. Somehow, seeing the fuzzy gray image of her daughter changed everything. She had a connection—something she had tried hard not to feel in the past, but was now lodged firmly in her heart.

She realized something else in that moment. She realized that giving her child up for adoption would mean giving away a part of herself—a part of her heart.

Back at the Hamilton Media office, Melissa tried to immerse herself in her work, but she found herself daydreaming about the baby. Her baby. Her daughter. What would she look like when she was born? Would she have her mother's blond hair, or would her hair be black like Dean's? Would her eyes be blue or hazel? Would she be a good baby, or would she be fussy?

While she hadn't quite finished filling out the adoption plan Richard had given her, Melissa now knew she would have to make some changes in it. She wanted to see her baby. She wanted to spend time with her before she gave her up. Each of those things was likely to make it more difficult to go through with the adoption. Was she only making it harder on herself?

Unable to concentrate on the files that needed sorting, Melissa picked up the phone and rang Amy's office. When her sister picked up, Melissa jumped in with her question.

"Amy, this is Melissa. You mentioned someone here had recently adopted a baby with Richard's help. Can you tell me who it is?"

"Of course. It's Karen Umber in advertising. She said she would be happy to talk with you anytime. How have you been?"

"I've been good. Things are settling down. I don't feel quite as unsettled as I did when I first came home. Richard and his family have made me feel welcome. You know, I've never been responsible for anyone but myself. It has been an eye-opener trying to keep tabs on two active girls."

"Sounds like it has been good for you."

"You're right. It has."

After talking to her sister for a few more minutes, Melissa hung up and rang Karen Umber's office. She got the voice mail. She left a brief message. It was barely five minutes later when her phone rang.

"Melissa, this is Karen. I'm sorry I missed your call, but I was on the phone with a new client. What can I do for you?"

"Thanks for ringing back so quickly. I know my sister told you that I'm thinking of adoption. Would you have a few minutes to answer some questions?"

"Of course. You can come to my office now, if you like."

"That would be great."

A few minutes later, Melissa entered one of the many small offices at the *Dispatch*. The room was narrow and crowded with an enormous desk overflowing with stacks of papers. Several large framed photos of a grinning baby boy decorated the top of a large filing cabinet.

Karen, a short, plump woman in her early thirties

dressed neatly in a tailored plum suit, rose from behind the desk. "Melissa, I'm so glad you've come. I'm always happy to show off Gavin's pictures and to brag about him. Please, sit down."

Melissa sat in a straight-back chair beside the desk. "Thank you for seeing me."

"Certainly. First, let me tell you how brave and selfless you are to be thinking about adoption. For those of us who can't have children, women like you are a blessing I can't begin to describe. Now, this is my boy." She handed Melissa a small photo album. Together they looked through the pictures with Karen pointing out her favorites.

"Your son is beautiful," Melissa said when she closed the book.

"Thanks. What questions can I answer for you?"

"I have so many. I don't know where to start."

"Of course. Let me tell you a little bit about my experience. My husband and I tried for six years without success to have children. About four years ago we began to look into adoption. Richard and I belong to the same church and when he heard we were thinking along those lines, he put us in touch with his friend who owns an adoption agency."

"Did you have to wait a long time?"

"No, we were blessed. We were chosen by a young woman about eighteen months after we got on the list."

"Does she see Gavin?"

"Yes. She has been to see him three times in the past year."

"Isn't that hard?"

"I'm sure it is for her, but Peggy has such a good outlook. She knows that Gavin is happy and healthy and she also knows that she wasn't ready to raise a child. She was sixteen. At the time she became pregnant she was living at home. Her mother wasn't well. Peggy was taking care of her, working and going to school at night. Her life still isn't easy, but she knows she made the right choice."

"Were you in the delivery room?"

"No, but Peggy allowed us to be in the waiting room. We saw Gavin when he was about an hour old. I tell you, my heart just melted at the sight of that boy. I couldn't love him more if I tried."

"I guess my biggest fear is that my baby will go to someone who isn't fit to be a parent."

"I can understand that. Let me tell you about the kind of screening we had to go through to adopt."

"Would you? I think that might help."

"Certainly, but I'd like to say one thing and I hope you don't think this is out of line. Please be sure in your heart that you can go through with this before you choose a couple. I know someone who was chosen twice, but both times the birth mothers backed out and decided to keep their babies. It is devastating to get that news."

Thirty minutes later, Melissa left Karen's office feeling more confident than ever that she was making the right decision. She had it within her power to give someone a child they longed for desperately. If she could find a couple like Karen and her husband, Melissa knew her baby would have a good life. That was what she wanted more than anything.

Her certainty lasted only a few hours. Late that night, as she lay under the quilt in her bedroom at Richard's, her doubts began to surface one by one. What was it about the wee hours of the night that made life seem so overwhelming?

Melissa rolled to her side and flipped her pillow, seeking a cool place for her cheek. Karen Umber's gratitude for the choice a young girl made was heartfelt and touching, but Melissa wasn't looking for gratitude.

She pressed a hand to her tummy. Until the sonogram this morning she had thought of her pregnancy as an unwanted problem. Now, thoughts of her baby filled her with warmth and tenderness.

"I think I love you," she whispered in the darkness. "I wish that were enough."

What if I kept you?

What if she did? How could she make it work? Melissa rolled to her other side, pulling the quilt to her chin. Keeping her baby would mean moving back home. It would also mean facing her father's disapproval day in and day out. What kind of life would that be for a baby?

Perhaps her mother was right and her father would come around in time. Maybe he would become a loving and cheerful grandfather, the kind every kid deserved. She could see herself working at the paper while her mother watched the baby. Wouldn't her mother's housekeeper, Vera Mae, be tickled to have a new baby to help raise?

Just the thought of Vera Mae's ample arms holding a baby was enough to make Melissa grin. Someday her daughter would be big enough to beg treats from the housekeeper and to dig into the wide pockets of her oversize apron for the pieces of candy Vera Mae kept stashed there for just that reason.

Richard would come to visit. He would hold the baby and tell her how pretty she was. He might even go with them when Melissa took the baby out in the stroller. They would look like an ordinary family walking along the path that circled the lake in Sugar Tree Park. He would make a wonderful father for her little girl.

Melissa's musings came to an abrupt halt. What was she doing? She was barely out of one foolhardy relationship. How could she be thinking about another? While it was true that she hadn't loved Dean and that their relationship had been over long before he left her, she had no business thinking about Richard in that way. The dream was tempting—only, it was based on wishful thinking and nothing more.

She rolled over, determined to get some sleep, but her stomach rumbled loudly. She was hungry again. It seemed that her baby was intent on having a fat mother. She threw back the covers and got out of bed. Pulling her pale blue-and-white embroidered robe over her blue plaid cotton pajamas, Melissa left her room and headed for the kitchen. If she couldn't sleep, she might as well raid the fridge. Anything was better than lying in bed and dreaming about an impossible life with Richard.

Determined to think about something else, she walked quickly down the hall and through the dining room. As she rounded the corner into the kitchen, she came face-to-face with the man she couldn't get out of her mind.

Chapter Twelve

Richard nearly dropped his bowl of ice cream when Melissa came barreling into the kitchen and almost into his arms. Her sudden appearance when he had spent the last several hours thinking about nothing but her was unnerving.

With a squeak, she jumped back and pressed a hand to her throat. "Gracious, Richard, you scared me to death. What are you doing in here?"

There was no point in telling her that she had invaded his dreams and kept him from sleeping. "I came in for a snack. What are you doing up?"

"I'm starving and I couldn't sleep, either. What do you have there?" She rose on tiptoe to peek into his bowl.

"Two scoops of Double Chocolate Chip Delight." He moved it away from the hungry glint in her eyes.

"Oh, no you don't." She reached out and plucked the bowl from his hands.

"Hey, get your own." He reached for his treat but she turned aside, blocking his move.

"This is definitely not on your diet. Ice cream is loaded with fat and sugar."

He tried reaching around her. "That's what makes it taste good. Give it here. I'll run an extra mile in the morning."

She moved the bowl behind her back. "You can run an extra mile without the ice cream. It will do you a lot more good. You have to take care of yourself. If you don't, who will?"

"You, apparently."

"I have to do something to repay you for giving me a place to stay. I'm sure there's some wonderfully crunchy celery in the fridge."

She looked adorable. Without makeup, her hair mussed and her bare toes peeking from beneath the hem of her robe, she seemed even younger than twenty-three. Her grin said she knew she was winning the argument.

"Give it back, Melissa."

"Or what?" She took a step backward as he advanced.

"Or you may need to find yourself another place to live."

"Ha! You wouldn't dare. Samantha and Lauren would be up in arms, not to mention Aunt Lettie."

"Don't tempt me. Two scoops of Double Chocolate Chip Delight might be worth the pain."

She had backed into the counter and could retreat no farther. He loomed before her, his arms crossed as he tried to maintain a stern expression. It wasn't easy.

"You leave me no choice. I'll just have to remove the temptation." She twisted around and began to spoon ice cream into her mouth.

"Hey!" He grabbed her shoulders and spun her back

to face him. She had a smear of ice cream across her lips. All thought of food left his head. All he wanted was to kiss her.

Her smile faded as she gazed at him and her eyes darkened. He leaned toward her. She closed her eyes and tilted her head back waiting for him. A breath away from her lips his conscience kicked in.

Don't take advantage of her, he chided himself. *She's the daughter of your friend. She's confused and searching for answers in her life. This may be what* you *want, but it isn't what* she *needs.*

Instead of kissing her, he used his thumb to wipe the cream from her lower lip. Her eyes flew open. He clearly read the confusion in them. She looked away. He wished he could offer some kind of excuse for his behavior, but nothing came to mind.

"You win, kid," he said at last. "The ice cream is yours, but don't expect me to munch celery while I watch you eat it."

Her chin came up and she managed a strained smile. "In that case, I'll take it to my room and eat it there. You won't get more when I leave, will you?"

"No. Like I said, you win."

She stepped around him, but paused and looked back. "Funny, it doesn't feel like I won."

He had no answer for that.

Melissa fled to her room. As the ice cream melted untouched in the bowl on her bedside table, she huddled on the bed and buried her face in her hands. She called herself every kind of fool.

It must have been blatantly obvious that she wanted him to kiss her. For one wonderful moment she thought he was going to. Then nothing—nothing but embarrassment as he tried to make light of her horrible blunder. What must he think of her? Of course he would think she was a loose woman. She had certainly provided him with proof of that by running away with Dean and coming home pregnant and unmarried. How could she face him again?

She wrapped her arms around her knees and stared at the wall. She didn't have to face him. She could leave. Her sister, Amy, would take her in.

Melissa scrambled off the bed and hurried to the closet. From its depths, she pulled out her only piece of luggage. She unzipped it on the bed and turned to the dresser. Pulling open the top drawer, she scooped up handfuls of underwear and dropped them in the suitcase. She yanked open the next drawer with such force that the entire thing came out. Her clothes and the drawer fell to the floor in a heap.

She looked at the mess, then at herself in the beveled mirror over the dresser. "What am I doing?"

Sinking cross-legged onto the floor, Melissa threaded her fingers through her hair and cradled her head in her hands. "I'm running away, that's what I'm doing."

If she left here it wouldn't be to go to Amy's. She would simply keep on going, stopping someplace new only until things became difficult, then running again. When would she find the courage to stop?

Now. Tonight.

What did it matter what Richard thought of her? Okay, it did matter, but the world wouldn't come to an end because an old, unrequited crush made her act like a flirtatious teenager.

There was much more at stake here than her wounded pride. Angela and Dave depended on her to help take care of the girls. She had promised to help Samantha with voice lessons. She had a job. She had a baby to think about.

She righted the dresser drawer beside her and began to replace her clothes. She would face Richard with her chin up and pretend it didn't matter that he hadn't kissed her.

"Besides, it's his loss," she declared, feeling a new resolve lift her spirits.

"So I'm suffering from a little rebound infatuation with the first guy that's been nice to me since Dean dumped me in Detroit. So what? I'll get over it. I'm done running away from my mistakes. From now on, I'm going to face them head-on."

The next morning, Melissa was already seated at the table in the breakfast nook, looking out the wide bay window at colorful chrysanthemums, pansies and hardy ageratum in the garden, when Angela shuffled in to put on the coffee.

"You're up bright and early," Angela mumbled, covering a yawn with one hand as she spooned grounds into a paper filter.

"I'm eager to get started on my research about your aunt Lettie and other women reporters of her era."

"I think it's wonderful that you're trying to bring their contributions to light."

"I like research. I like finding old facts that have been overlooked."

"I remember that great paper you did for my class on Southern women writers."

"Do you? That seems like a lifetime ago."

Angela moved to the sink and began filling the pot with water. "Have you thought about going back to school?"

"I've thought about it, but, as sad as this is for Wallace Hamilton's daughter to say, I can't afford it."

"There are programs to help with cost. You should look into it. We have a new work study program for single parents at the college. One of the professors was saying just the other day that she was hoping to find a research assistant."

"I know about the program. I was there when Felicity Simmons interviewed the dean, but you forget, I'm not going to be a single parent for more than a day or two. After that, I'll be a birth mother with limited visitation."

"I'm sorry. This must be hard for you to talk about. I never quite know what to say."

"It doesn't bother me to talk about it. It doesn't feel real yet. I assume that will change as the time gets closer."

"Are you sure that adoption is what you want?" She poured the water into the reservoir and turned the brew cycle on.

"You can't imagine it, can you?"

Angela sent Melissa an embarrassed look over her shoulder. She turned around and stuffed her hands in the pockets of her robe. The gesture reminded Melissa of Richard. He often did the same thing when confronting a difficult situation.

"Am I that transparent?" Angela managed to look sheepish and apologetic at the same time.

"A little."

"I'm sorry. You're right. I can't imagine giving up one of my girls."

She held up one hand. "Okay, I will admit that there are days I think about taking them to the pound and exchanging them for a puppy, but in reality, I can't envision myself without them."

She laid her hand over her heart. "They are like the air I breathe. I need them to make me whole."

"That's what I like to believe I will be doing. My baby will make some woman who has been waiting for a child feel whole. At least, I try to think of it like that." She couldn't admit the truth out loud. No matter how hard she tried to convince herself that she was doing the right thing, it still didn't feel as though she was.

"I admire your courage."

"Now, that is one thing I'm sure I don't have. But I'm working on it."

"I think you have far more courage than you know."

"Let's hope you're right."

Their conversation came to a halt as other members of the family began straggling in. Dave came in first. He gave his wife a peck on the cheek.

"No coffee yet?"

"Another minute, dear."

Close behind Dave was Samantha. "Morning. What's for breakfast?"

"Cereal. I don't have time to cook this morning. I've got an early staff meeting." Angela opened a cupboard and pulled out a box.

"Cereal again," Samantha moaned as she plunked down beside Melissa. Lauren came in, looking more than half-asleep, and slipped into a chair. She crossed her arms on the table and laid her head on them.

"Unless your father wants to cook, yes," Angela

declared, switching her mug to replace the glass pot and filling her husband's mug from the half-full carafe.

Lauren muttered, "Don't give Dad a skillet. He's *so* dangerous."

"I set the bacon on fire one time. One time! And I get grief for it the rest of my life." Dave rolled his eyes and Melissa smothered a laugh.

Lauren opened one eye to peek at Melissa. "It was twice," she whispered, "but he made me promise not to tell Mom about the second time."

Melissa winked. "Your secret is safe with me."

She was still trying not to laugh when Richard wandered in, looking as if he hadn't slept at all. Her heart rolled over at the sight of his tousled hair and bleary eyes.

It was only a leftover crush or a rebound infatuation, she told herself. She wasn't falling for him. She wouldn't repay his kindness by putting him in the awkward position of having to fend off her unwelcome advances.

She managed a bright smile for him, but it was Angela, handing out cereal bowls, who took the words out of Melissa's mouth. "Richard, you look like something the cat dragged in."

"Thanks, sis. Good morning to you, too."

She stood on tiptoe to plant a kiss on his cheek. "I'd love to stay and talk, but I've got to get dressed and run. Girls, I'll be home late. Be good for Melissa."

"We will," Samantha said, pouring herself a bowl of flakes before passing the box to Lauren.

Angela waved as she hurried out. Richard poured himself a cup of coffee, then stood at the counter beside his brother-in-law. "What are your plans for tonight?"

Dave dragged a hand down his goatee. "I've got two houses that need their final electrical inspections today but they are on the same side of the county. If all goes well, I should be done by five o'clock. Maybe I can pick up supper on my way home. What would you girls like?"

Lauren shot up out of her trance. "Pizza!"

"Tacos!" Samantha cried.

Dave shook his head. "Melissa, what would you like?"

"Me? Steamed broccoli, or maybe pickled beets. Oh, I know—dill pickles and pistachio ice cream."

"Ugh." Lauren looked at her in disbelief.

Dave and Richard were giving her the same kind of look.

Melissa glanced from one man to the other. "I'm kidding, y'all."

"Oh, good." Dave put down his empty cup. "For a minute there, I was having flashbacks to my wife's last pregnancy. With Lauren, all she wanted was guacamole."

Melissa wrinkled her nose. "I never really liked the stuff. I hope I don't start craving it."

Richard tipped his head to the side. "Hmm, I hope you do. I love the stuff."

"You would, because it's loaded with calories."

"Avocados are a vegetable. I distinctly remember my doctor telling me I could have all the vegetables I wanted. Even baked potatoes."

She crossed her arms. "As long as you leave off the sour cream. Besides, avocados are a fruit. Don't you have an extra mile to run this morning?"

He raised his coffee cup in a half salute. "Nope, I passed up all the sweet stuff last night."

She looked down and cupped her hands around her

mug of tea. Was he referring to their almost kiss? No, of course not. He was talking about ice cream. Still, she couldn't stop the faint flutter of hope that skidded sideways through her chest. It would be nice if he thought of her as sweet stuff.

When Melissa arrived at her desk in the Hamilton Media building, she dropped off her purse and her jacket before heading down to the archive vaults. She had half an hour to look through the microfilm rolls before she had to start working. It wasn't much time, but she could at least narrow her search to the years Lettie had been employed by the paper and expand from that later. She hadn't yet asked Ed Bradshaw if she could pursue the story on company time. First, she wanted to make sure she had the facts to back up her idea.

When she came up from the basement twenty-eight minutes later, she was surprised to see Tim, Amy and Heather standing in front of her desk. From the look on their faces, something was wrong. She could think of only one thing. Her dad.

Tim caught sight of her first. "Where have you been?" he demanded.

"In the basement. Is it Dad? Has something happened?" She looked from him to her sisters.

Amy came forward and took her hand. "Dad is fine."

"Until he sees this," Tim added. He handed Melissa a folded copy of the paper.

Melissa was totally confused. "I don't understand."

"Look at the paper," Heather said gently.

Melissa opened the copy she held. It wasn't the *Dispatch,* it was this morning's copy of the *Observer.*

She blinked twice before she could be sure of what she saw. There on the front page were a pair of pictures. One was of her with Dean outside a Nashville nightclub taken some time at the beginning of the summer. The other one had to have been taken yesterday. It was a picture of her and Richard leaving Dr. Miller's maternity clinic. The caption below the pictures read, Punk Rocker or Debonair Attorney—Who Fathered Unwed Hamilton Heiress's Baby?

Aghast, Melissa sank into the corner of her desk. "They make it look like Richard and I are…"

"Are having an affair," Tim finished.

"We aren't. We never." She stumbled over the words as she struggled to regain her composure. She looked at each of her siblings in turn. "Richard has been nothing but kind to me. Who would smear his name like this?"

"A better question might be, who knows you are pregnant?" Heather asked.

"No one outside of our family and Richard's family. I can't believe this." Melissa couldn't take her eyes off the photo of Richard. He was smiling down at her and she was grinning at him as if they shared some great secret. Of course they had both been amazed and excited by seeing the baby on the sonogram. That's all it was. Why would someone at the *Observer* try to turn it into something dirty?

She knew the answer. Because dirt sold papers. Suddenly, she surged to her feet. "Daddy can't find out like this. I have to get to the hospital. I have to see him."

"I'll take you."

She whirled around to see Richard walking toward

her. He held a copy of the same paper in his hand. "Oh, Richard, I'm so sorry about this."

"It isn't your fault."

"How can you say that? I've dragged your name down in the mud with my own willfulness and foolish behavior. Please forgive me."

Amy laid a hand on Melissa's shoulder. "The only people down in the mud are the ones trying to make money off your situation."

Richard stopped beside Tim and the two men shared a look. Richard said, "When I find out who's behind this, I intend to see that they are exposed for the malicious cowards they truly are."

"You can expect the full support and resources of the family to back you up."

"Thanks."

Richard reached for Melissa and took her by the arm. His grip was firm but gentle. She sensed his anger but he managed to keep it in check. "My car is outside. I'll take you to see your father. I'm sure he'll have a few words for me, too."

At the hospital, Melissa walked quickly with Richard from the parking lot toward the wide entrance. As she drew nearer, her steps lagged until her feet seemed to be rooted in the pavement. The sight of those doors had made her weak with terror. Richard took her hand and squeezed it.

"Courage, Melissa."

"I can't do this."

"What do you see?"

"I see Jenny gasping for breath. I can't breathe, either."

"Yes, you can. Look at me."

She did, happy to avert her eyes from the building.

His eyes were serious, unsmiling, filled with determination. "Take a deep breath."

"I can't."

"Yes, you can. Do as I say."

He had never spoken to her like this. She took a step back, but he held her hand.

"Jenny isn't here. Your father is here, and he needs you."

"I know. Only…I can't."

"Look at that building."

"I don't want to."

"Just look at it," he coaxed.

She turned her eyes.

"Why are you here?"

"Because I don't want Daddy to find out about my pregnancy from that stupid paper."

"Why not?"

She looked at him in confusion. "Because it will hurt him."

"Good. Do you love your father?"

"Of course I do."

"Then you are going to see him. I know you are frightened, but I'm here. I'll be with you every step of the way."

Swallowing hard, Melissa managed to nod. Richard slipped his arm across her shoulders and drew her close to his side. She leaned into his strength and tried to absorb some of it into herself.

"One small step at a time, Melissa. That's all the Lord is asking of you."

"He's got big expectations."

She felt Richard shake with a silent chuckle. "You're up to them, Melissa. I believe in you."

More than anything, she found she didn't want to let him down. Richard believed in her. If he believed, perhaps she could, too. "One small step, right?"

"Right."

Together they began to move toward the hospital. Melissa closed her eyes as they neared the door. She didn't care how it looked to others. She leaned on Richard, trusting him to guide her. She felt the rush of air as the outside doors slid open and then they were inside. Her knees were trembling.

"You've got it, sweetheart," he whispered. "The elevators are just ahead."

Once they were inside the lift, she managed to open her eyes. Fortunately, they were alone. "Thank you. I never would have made it this far without you."

"That's what friends are for."

Friends. Yes, he was her friend and so much more. How could she ever repay him?

The elevator doors slid open. Melissa looked down the long hall and knew that her fear would not hold her back after having come this far. She stepped out with Richard still at her side. Off to the left was a small waiting area with vending machines. She turned to Richard and laid a hand on his chest. "I'm all right now. Would you mind waiting here? I should do this alone."

"Are you sure?"

"No, but I'm going to do it anyway."

"All right. I'll be here until you send for me. He's in the last room on the left."

"Thanks."

Melissa walked down the hall knowing he was watching her. At the room he had indicated, she pushed open the door and paused inside. Her father was lying quietly on the hospital bed with his eyes closed.

He had aged. How could he not, with all that he had gone through? Now she was here to add to those burdens. She walked in and stood at the foot of his bed. Her hands were shaking, she realized, and she clasped them tightly around her purse.

"Hello, Daddy," she said quietly.

Her father's eyes flew open, wide with surprise, then narrowed in a glare. Her newfound courage wavered sharply.

"It's about time you came to see your old man."

"I know and I'm sorry. That sounds lame, but I mean it. I'm sorry I haven't been here before. May I sit down?"

"Suit yourself."

She came around the end of the bed and sat down at the foot.

"If you came because of this, you could have saved yourself a trip." He tossed a rolled-up copy of the *Observer* toward her. "So you're pregnant. Like them, I find myself wondering who the father might be. Do you even know?"

Mortified beyond belief, she closed her eyes to shut out the sight of his angry face. "I'm sorry, Daddy. I didn't want you to find out like this."

"It's that musician, isn't it?"

"Yes," she answered, her voice so small she wondered if he heard.

"Melissa, where did I go wrong with you?"

"I've made a lot of mistakes, but I'm trying to turn my life around."

"How? By having your picture smeared on the front page of that rag?"

"You know I had nothing to do with that."

"It's bad enough that you embarrassed me, but think about your mother."

"Mom knows about my pregnancy. She's supporting me."

"Giving you money, you mean."

"No, not money. She's giving me moral support while I figure things out."

"Well, you're not planning on keeping the child, I hope. If you haven't got enough sense and moral fiber to keep from getting pregnant in the first place, you've got no business trying to raise a child."

"That's a little like the pot calling the kettle black, isn't it? I've read a few things about you lately, too."

"You watch what you say to me, Melissa Hamilton."

"No. I don't think I will. I dreaded coming to see you because I knew exactly how you would react. Like this. Everyone said to give you the benefit of the doubt, but they were wrong."

She rose to her feet. "I'm done being afraid of disappointing you. I had planned to give my baby up for adoption. Do you want to know why? Because I knew that's what you would expect me to do.

"It's a girl, in case you were wondering. But I don't want to give her up. I want to keep her, and love her till the end of my life, so I'm going to disappoint you one more time, Daddy. I'm keeping this baby. And I'm going to raise her without any help from you!"

Tears blurred her vision as she turned and fled the room. She heard her father calling after her, but she didn't stop. She had to get away. Down the hall, Richard stepped out of the waiting room beside the elevators. Melissa turned blindly toward the exit door at the stairs. She didn't want Richard to see her like this. She didn't want him or anyone trying to talk her out of her decision.

She darted out the door, but not quick enough. She heard him calling her. "Melissa, wait!"

"Leave me alone," she shouted. She glanced back over her shoulder to see him coming after her. Blinded by her tears, she misjudged the next step. Suddenly, she was falling.

Chapter Thirteen

Horrified, Richard watched Melissa fall. He reached for her, but she was too far away. Like a puppet with severed strings she tumbled down the steps and came to rest, unmoving, at the bottom of the landing.

Dear God, no!

With his heart hammering painfully in his chest, he rushed to her side. "Melissa, can you hear me?"

She moaned. To his relief, she opened her eyes, although she quickly squeezed them shut as a grimace of pain contorted her face.

Richard gently swept her hair out of her face. Her cheek was already darkening with a bruise. Blood trickled from a scrape on her temple. "Don't try to move. Where does it hurt?"

She held her left hand clutched close to her chest. "That was so clumsy of me."

"Never mind that, tell me what hurts." With hands that shook slightly, he palpated her legs.

She struggled to sit up. He tried to stop her with a hand on her shoulder, but she cried out.

His gut clenched in dread. "What's wrong?"

She grabbed his hand and looked at him with fear-filled eyes. "I think I hurt the baby."

"Don't move. I'm going to get help."

"Please, hurry."

"I'll be right back." He hated leaving her, but he had no choice. He pulled open the nearest door and stepped out into the corridor. The large giraffe and lion on the wall told him it was the Pediatric Ward. He ran down the hall to the nurses' station. One look at his face and his breathless explanation sent the women there into immediate action. Help came from every direction in a matter of minutes.

Richard stood back out of the way as the hospital staff, led by a young doctor, examined Melissa, then transferred her to a gurney and headed toward the emergency rooms. Picking up her purse from where it was lodged in the corner, he followed behind them. All the way to the E.R. the same phrase kept running over and over in his mind.

Please let Melissa be all right, Lord, and please let her baby be unharmed.

As the staff whisked her into an empty trauma room, he was stopped from following by one of the nurses. "I'm sorry, you'll have to wait out here."

He nodded his understanding, too upset to speak. She closed the door, shutting him out. He listened to the murmur of low voices inside, wishing he had the right to be at Melissa's side. Up until the second he saw her plunging down the stairs just beyond his reach, he had no idea how much he loved her. Now, he couldn't believe that he had deluded himself into thinking his affection was only friendship.

He loved everything about her. He loved the way she made him smile. He loved the sound of her laughter. He loved the way her chin came up when she was ready to argue with him. He loved the way she struggled so valiantly to turn her life around. She might not believe in herself, but he believed in her.

Just then, he heard the sound of weeping coming through the closed door. He leaned his head against the wall and squeezed his eyes shut as hot tears stung them.

Please, Lord, I'm begging You to spare the life of Melissa's unborn child. You know Melissa's heart. You know that she loves this baby. Please, don't let it end like this.

How long he stood outside praying for the woman he loved, he had no idea. Finally, the door opened and the young doctor looked out. "Are you Richard?"

He looked up, hopeful yet fearful at the same time. "Yes."

"She'd like you to come in."

"How is she?"

"She has a few bruises and a possible sprain. We'll know more in a little while. Come in." The doctor stepped aside.

"Thank you." Richard tried to brace himself for bad news as he stepped inside the bright white room. Melissa lay on a narrow bed with her face turned toward the wall. Another nurse finished taking her blood pressure and stuffed the black cuff into a wire holder on the wall. When both of the staff left the room, Richard crossed to Melissa's side. She lay still, looking pale and sad. Her left hand rested on a pillow beside her. The right hand she held splayed over her stomach.

"Lissa, I'm here."

She turned her tear-streaked face toward him. She had a bandage taped over the cut on her forehead. Her cheek showed a large bruise, and her knuckles on one hand were red and swollen. In spite of her battered appearance, she managed a weak smile for him. "Amy is the only one who calls me Lissa."

"I'm sorry."

"No, it's okay. I always liked it."

"How are you?"

"Banged up. They're going to x-ray my wrist. The doctor thinks it's only a sprain but he wants to be sure."

Richard laid his hand over her uninjured one. He wanted to ask about the baby, but the words stuck in his throat. What if her little life had been snuffed out? He couldn't bear to think of it.

Melissa curled her fingers around his and held tight. "They're going to do a sonogram to see…to see if everything is all right. The doctor couldn't…couldn't hear her heartbeat, but he said that wasn't unusual this early in the pregnancy. They heard it yesterday. Do you think he was lying to me?"

"No. I'm sure he wasn't."

She tipped her head back. Tears streamed from the corners of her eyes. "I didn't want to be pregnant. I didn't want a baby. I tried so hard not to feel the love that kept creeping into my heart. And now she might be dead…and no one will ever have loved her."

"Oh, sweetheart, don't do this to yourself." He leaned down and laid his cheek against hers. He felt the dampness of her tears. She circled his neck with one arm and held him close.

"Lissa, you have always loved your baby," he whispered. "I've seen it in your eyes. I've heard it in your voice. I know it by the way you touch her when you talk about her. You've held her under your heart all these months. You wanted to give her the best life possible even if that meant someone else would raise her. Who could be loved more than that?"

"I do love her. I do. I don't want to lose her now. Will you ask God to let me keep her? He might listen to you. You're such a good man."

"I've been praying for her and for you. You can pray, too, Melissa. He will hear you."

"I don't know how."

"Just say what is in your heart. I wish I could promise you that God will do as we ask, but I can't. We have to accept His will. We have to hold on to the love He has for us and use it to find the strength we need to face whatever comes. He loves you and He loves your baby. And if He wants her to come home with Him, it's because He has the most glorious place for her at His side." His tears mixed with hers as they held each other tight.

Behind them, the door opened. Richard straightened from his awkward position, reluctant to move away. A young woman in pink scrubs pushed a sonogram machine into the room. He looked down at Melissa. "I'd better wait outside."

Melissa knew she couldn't let go of Richard's hand. He was her anchor. She needed his strength, his faith to help her. "No. Don't go. Stay. In case…you know…in case—"

"Hush. Of course I'll stay, if you want me."

"I do. I need you."

Together they waited until the sonogram technician set up her machine. Melissa closed her eyes and held on to Richard's hand as she began to pray for the first time in years.

Please, Lord, I know that I haven't been the person You wanted me to be. If You'll just give me another chance I know that I can do better. I love my baby, my little Jenny. I want to see her face. I want to hear her laugher. I want to tell her all about the special girl she's named after.

But if You do take her to heaven, please let her spend time with my friend Jen. I know Jen is with You and I know she'll take good care of my baby girl.

The wand with its cold gel was laid on Melissa's stomach. The machine came on. She held her breath until the static-filled sound settled into rapid, beautiful beats. Joy, sharp as an electric jolt, shot through her. She opened her eyes and looked at Richard. He grinned at her and she knew he shared her happiness. She focused for the first time on the woman running the machine. "That's her, isn't it?"

"Yes. We have a good strong heartbeat and someone is kicking at my wand."

"Does that mean she's okay?"

"Everything looks good."

Melissa nearly wept with happiness. "Thank you. And thank You, God."

The woman unplugged her machine and left the room leaving them alone. Richard squeezed Melissa's hand between both of his and raised them to his lips. He bowed his head and his voice shook slightly as he spoke.

"Thank You, dear Lord, for hearing our prayers this day. Thank You."

His relief was so palpable, his words of thanks so heartfelt and sincere that Melissa suddenly saw beyond a shadow of a doubt that she loved him.

The emotion that filled her heart took her breath away. She loved him. With utter clarity, she saw that the feelings she once had for Dean were a mere shadow of what she felt now. How could she ever have mistaken what they had for love? It was like mistaking a shallow puddle for the ocean.

She studied every beloved angle and curve of Richard's face. When he opened his eyes, his gentle spirit was reflected there and beautiful to see.

The door to the room opened again and the young resident walked in with her chart in hand, followed by the nurse who had been in earlier. He said, "Mr. Hamilton, it looks like your baby is fine, but I'd like to keep Mrs. Hamilton overnight for observation."

"I'm not Mr. Hamilton, Doctor."

"Oh, I'm sorry. I thought you two were together."

"I'm a friend of Miss Hamilton's. A friend of the family, actually. In fact, I'm her attorney."

Melissa noticed the flush on Richard's cheeks. Poor man, this was the third time in two days that he had been mistaken for her baby's father. If only it were true.

But it wasn't. He was her friend. She managed a smile for the embarrassed young doctor as she pulled her hand free from Richard's grasp, and tucked her newfound love into a corner of her heart for safekeeping.

"Richard, could you call my mother?"

"Certainly," he said. "She'll want to be here. Excuse

me." He left the room with one backward glance before he closed the door. Did his eyes hold a look of regret, or did she only imagine it?

The young doctor lifted her injured hand. "I'm going to wrap up this wrist. I don't want you to use it for a few days." He was gentle, but it did hurt and her hand was throbbing madly when he finished.

He seemed to notice her distress. "I can get you something for the pain."

"Is it safe for the baby?"

"Certainly. I'll have the nurse bring you something."

As they left her alone again, Melissa closed her eyes. "Okay, little one, it's going to be just you and me. I'm going to make a good life for us. I promise."

Melissa agreed to spend the night, although she doubted that she would ever be comfortable in a hospital, but she was willing to do whatever it took to keep her unborn child safe. God had answered her frantic prayers for her little girl today, and Melissa vowed she would never again do anything to jeopardize her pregnancy.

Richard had seen to it that her family knew about her accident. Nora came, intending to spend the night by her side. All of Melissa's siblings, except Jeremy, had come and gone from her room by eight o'clock. It was nearing midnight, but Melissa couldn't sleep. She shifted her bruised hip and bandaged wrist into a more comfortable position in the bed.

"Do you need something?" her mother asked, sitting up from the light doze she had fallen into in the recliner.

"No, I'm fine. I'm sorry I woke you."

"One thing you will learn is that there really isn't any sleep to be had in a hospital."

"It must have been awful for you all these months with Dad so sick. I'm really, really sorry I wasn't there to help you."

"That's in the past, dear. You're home now and that is what counts."

"Have you talked to Daddy?"

"Of course. He's terribly upset about the way he spoke to you today. I hope you believe that."

Melissa tilted her head back and stared at the ceiling. "I do. I just wish that he and I could find a way to talk to each other without—I don't know—without hurting each other."

"That will come in time, I'm sure of it. He tried to get the doctor to let him come down and see you."

She looked at her mother. "He did?"

"Of course he did." Nora leaned forward to lay her hand on Melissa's arm.

"Why wouldn't the doctor let him come? I thought he was nearly ready to go home."

"I didn't want to worry you, but your father has been having a few heart irregularities. The doctors don't think it is serious, but they don't want him wandering around the hospital. I promised to update him on your condition every few hours. I'm sure he's impatiently waiting for me now."

"Poor Mom. We really put you in the middle, didn't we?"

"I'm exactly where I want to be in my life. Helping my family cope with whatever comes along."

"Have you heard from Jeremy?"

"Not for a few weeks. I worry about him. He was very hurt when he found out the truth. I don't blame him for wanting to know his father's parents. I just hope he finds some comfort there."

"I'm hoping that I can be half the mother that you are."

"Your father said that you intend to keep the baby. Is that true?"

Melissa splayed the fingers of her right hand over the lump in her tummy. "I do. I want to keep her."

"It's a girl?" Nora's eyes brightened.

Smiling, Melissa nodded. "That's what the sonogram said."

Her mother grinned. "A girl. Oh, they make the cutest baby clothes now. It will be so much fun having a granddaughter."

"You really are excited at the idea of being a grandmother?"

"Darling, I won't lie to you. I was very disappointed when I found out you were pregnant. I had hoped that none of my children would make the same mistakes I made. I had so many dreams for you. I wanted you to have a career that excited you. I've dreamed about the kind of wedding you would have. I love you and I want only the best for you, but sometimes things happen. Then we have to face what is and not dwell on what is lost." She gently tucked a strand of Melissa's hair behind her ear.

"To answer your question, yes, I am very excited about having a grandchild. A baby is a most wondrous gift."

Richard found himself facing another sleepless night, tossing and turning as he relived the moment of Melissa falling just beyond his reach. It took all his willpower not to go driving back to the hospital to make sure she and the baby were still doing okay. She had her family with her. That was who she needed, not him.

He had had to relate the story first to Dave and the girls and then again to Angela when she got home. Everyone was concerned, but he convinced them not to race to the medical center by telling them Melissa needed her rest. It was something he got little of that night. Finally, after what seemed like an eternity, he watched the sky begin to lighten outside his window.

Rising, he dressed for his run, knowing it was useless to try and sleep. Once outside in the crisp morning air, he felt as if he could think at last. His feet found their rhythm on the deserted streets and the words he had been skirting around all night rolled though his mind.

He was in love with Melissa. He wanted to share her life, to be a father to her child. He wanted so much to tell her of his love, but he was unsure what his next move should be. Even if she cared for him, and he had some hope that she did, he knew he had to be patient.

Perhaps it was a bit old-fashioned, but he found himself wanting Wallace's blessing before he made his feelings known to Melissa. The last thing he wanted was to add another wedge between her and her father.

He had known Wallace since his early days as a struggling attorney. He had been awed that the man behind Hamilton Media had taken an interest in his career after he successfully negotiated a tricky labor settlement for the dockworkers in Hickory Mills. In spite of their age difference, the two men had formed a firm friendship. Wallace's respect was something Richard didn't want to jeopardize.

By the end of his five miles, the fresh air had helped

clear his head. He was certain that he had worked out
the best way to proceed. He would feel out Wallace on
the issue. He didn't really think her father would object,
but there was an age difference that might matter.

The main thing was not to rush Melissa with his
feelings. Her life was already filled with turmoil. He
would give her time to settle into motherhood and into
life in the community. Like himself, she had turned to
God and prayed for her baby yesterday. Richard
believed it was a start toward Melissa finding her faith
again. He easily saw himself coaxing her into attending
church with him and his family and helping her redis-
cover God's grace.

Satisfied with his plan, Richard walked into the
house feeling happy and hopeful. He would bide his
time, giving both Melissa and himself a chance to let
their affections mature.

He took a quick shower, then called the hospital and
was put though to Melissa's room. Her mother answered
and her hushed tone had him worried until she reassured
him Melissa was simply sleeping. Nora informed him of
her plan to stay at the hospital until Melissa was released
and then take her to Richard's home. Heather had volun-
teered to stay with her sister for the remainder of the afternoon or until Angela got home. With that worry taken
care of, he hung up and set about getting ready for work.

It wasn't until nearly two o'clock in the afternoon that
he was able to get away to the hospital once more. As
he approached Wallace's room, he saw the door partway
open and heard the sound of raised voices. Wallace apparently had a visitor. Richard was about to retreat to the
waiting room, when he overheard his own name.

"McNeil sent me a letter, that's how I know what's going on. Melissa convinced me you wouldn't give one penny to help her, but I think you'll pay up when you hear what I have to say."

"You miserable cad! You took advantage of my daughter. Why should I pay you anything?"

Chapter Fourteen

Richard frowned and stepped closer to the partially open door. He didn't recognize the other voice, but he couldn't mistake the threat it carried.

"I know how people like you Hamiltons think. You want to hush up her pregnancy and get rid of the kid. You don't want a constant reminder of how low your precious daughter has stooped. I did some checking after I got that letter from her attorney. She can't give the kid away unless I sign the adoption papers, too. For a small fee of say, ten thousand dollars, we can keep it all nice and friendly. I sign and then disappear. That's what you want, isn't it?"

"You think you can blackmail me? I'll have you tossed in jail so fast your head will spin," Wallace bellowed.

"How will that look to the press? I'm the kid's father. If you want me to go away, it's going to cost you, old man. Otherwise, I'll be the most devoted little daddy you ever saw. Melissa won't be able to turn around without bumping into me. I'll get joint custody. Think of it, old man, you're going to have to ask me if Junior can spend Christmas with you and yours."

"Get out!" Wallace's shout turned into a strangled gasp.

Richard pushed open the door. Wallace, his face ashen, was clutching his chest as he slid sideways in bed. Rushing to his friend, Richard caught hold of his shoulders. "Take it easy, Wallace. I'll get help."

"Can't...breathe."

Richard punched the call light. When no one answered, he snapped at Dean Orton, "Get a nurse."

Orton looked thunderstruck. He took a step toward the door. "I didn't do anything. The old man just keeled over."

"Nurse! I need a nurse," Richard yelled at the top of his lungs.

One of the staff appeared in the doorway. She hurried to Wallace's side. "What's going on here?"

"Mr. Hamilton is having chest pain."

"All right, step aside, please." One look at Wallace had her pushing the emergency call button on the wall over his bed. "Code Blue, Room 416."

In minutes the room filled up with people. A red crash cart was wheeled in and another nurse politely, but firmly, instructed Richard and Dean to leave.

Richard stepped outside in time to see Dr. Strickland racing down the hall, his white coattails flapping. "What happened?" he demanded as he sailed into the room. Richard didn't hear the nurse's answer.

The activity had drawn plenty of attention as both patients and families looked out of doorways to see what was happening. A burly security guard came toward Richard and stationed himself outside the door. Dean turned and began to walk quickly toward the exit sign at the stairwell.

Richard turned to the security guard and pointed at

Dean. "My name is Richard McNeil, I'm an attorney and I'd like that man detained."

"On what grounds, sir?"

"He was attempting to extort money from Mr. Hamilton before he collapsed."

The guard spoke into the radio at his shoulder. "Dispatch, get me the police department and get someone to the south stairwell to stop and hold a man in a red sweatshirt and black jeans. He has shoulder-length brown hair and a mustache."

To Richard, he said, "I'll need a statement, sir. Please wait here."

"I'm not going anywhere until I know how Wallace is doing."

"Richard, what's going on?"

He spun around at the sound of Nora's worried voice. She hurried toward him and grasped his arm.

"Wallace started to have chest pain a few minutes ago." Her eyes widened in fear. "Is it serious? Can I see him?"

"I don't know. Dr. Strickland is with him now. They asked me to leave the room. I think you should wait here."

It wasn't long before Wallace's physician stepped out into the hallway with them.

"Doctor, how is he?" Nora's voice quivered, but Richard was amazed at how composed she remained.

"I'm glad you are here, Nora. I'm going to transfer Wallace to our cardiac unit. I suspect he has suffered a mild heart attack. We won't know for sure how serious this is until we can do some additional testing. I've already contacted a cardiac specialist to see him."

"But he was doing so well. You said yourself that he would be able to come home in a few days."

"I know this is a blow. I simply can't tell you anything for sure just yet."

The door to Wallace's room opened and the hospital staff pushed his bed out. An oxygen mask covered his face and a small monitor bleeped beside him in the bed.

Nora covered her mouth with her fingers. "He's been through so much already. Dear Lord, how much more can he take?"

At the sound of her voice, Wallace opened his eyes. He managed a weak smile and lifted his hand. She clutched it between hers and walked by his side as they wheeled him down the hall.

Dr. Strickland studied Richard. "I understand there was some kind of altercation in the room before Wallace's attack. Care to tell me about it?"

"It's a matter I think will be better left to the police."

Dr. Strickland raised an eyebrow. "The police?"

"Rest assured, Doctor, I'll do my best to see that the individual never bothers any of the Hamiltons again."

Melissa was pretending to rest. She opened one eye to see Heather still sitting in a chair by the window reading. Beyond the drapes the sky was tinted with the red and gold of a glorious sunset. She had arrived at Richard's house just after noon and so far, any attempt on her part to get out of bed had been quickly squelched by Heather or Angela. The two of them could easily find jobs as prison guards. Melissa never knew her quiet sister could be such a bulldog.

Heather's cell phone rang. She threw Melissa an apologetic look, then spoke quietly. Melissa couldn't overhear the conversation, but she saw Heather become noticeably upset as she hurried out of the room. Melissa sat up and waited.

When her sister reentered a few minutes later, Melissa was determined to find out what was wrong. "Heather, what is it?"

A look of indecision flashed across Heather's face, but was gone in an instant. Meeting Melissa's eyes, she said, "Dad has had another setback."

"Oh, no!"

"He's stable for now, but he's in the cardiac unit. Apparently, they think he's had a minor heart attack. They're getting him ready for a heart catheter. Amy, Chris and Tim are with Mom."

Melissa threw back the quilt. "We should be there, too."

Heather planted herself in front of her sister. "You aren't going anywhere. Your doctor said bed rest for twenty-four hours."

Melissa chewed her lip in indecision. "I've neglected Mom and all of you for far too long. I should be there."

"Mom said you would say that. Her instructions are for me to keep you here by any means necessary."

She couldn't bring herself to ask if her argument with her father had brought this on. "Are you sure he's okay?"

"I only know what Mom told me."

Melissa settled back against the padded headboard. "You go. I'll be fine here. Angela and the girls will keep an eye on me. Tell Mom I'm doing just as I should, and she isn't to worry about me for a minute."

"Like that will make her stop worrying."

Melissa spread her hand on her tummy. "I think worry is what mothers do best. You go and call me with an update. I don't care how late it is. I'll stay in bed, but I won't sleep a wink until I know Daddy is okay."

"All right," Heather conceded. It was obvious she wanted to go to the hospital and just as obvious she thought she should stay.

Pulling the covers over her lap and smoothing them with deliberate care, Melissa sought a way to mollify her sister. "Why don't you see if Angela or one of the girls can sit with me for a while?"

"Are you sure?"

"I'll be fine. Go."

"Okay, but only if someone can sit with you." She left the room and a few minutes later she was back, not with Angela, but with Richard.

"Will I do?" he asked from the doorway. "Angela is making supper and Dave has taken the girls out to see the progress on the house. They should be back in half an hour. Angela thought keeping the girls out from underfoot was the best way to see you got some rest."

"You'll do in a pinch. Pull up a chair." Melissa tried to keep the happy skip of her heart from showing in her voice or on her face. Whenever he was near she felt an overwhelming sense of comfort and happiness.

Heather hovered near the door. Melissa shooed her with one hand. "Go! And let me know how Daddy is doing as soon as you hear anything new."

"Now you sound like Amy. No one would think I'm the older sister here. All right, I'm going." She headed out the door, leaving it open behind her.

Melissa watched Richard pull a chair up beside the bed. "Did you hear about Daddy?"

"I did. Actually, I was there when it happened."

He didn't quite meet her gaze. Something wasn't right. "What aren't you telling me?"

"I have strict instructions not to upset you."

"Is Daddy worse than Heather said?"

"No, it isn't that."

"Richard McNeil, you have not begun to see upset unless you tell me right this instant what you're hiding."

He glanced toward the door, then leaned forward, his elbows propped on his knees. "Dean is back in town."

"Dean is *from* Davis Landing. Why should it matter that he's back?"

"I wasn't sure how you would feel about that."

"I think if you told me there was a fly in my soup I'd feel about the same—annoyed and a little sick, but not crushed. How did you find out he was back?" She watched Richard take a deep breath. Suddenly, she wasn't sure she wanted to hear more.

"He went to see your father today."

"Dean went to see Daddy? Why?"

"He tried to force Wallace to pay him money."

"That doesn't make any sense. My pregnancy is front-page news. It's not like the family is trying to hide it."

"Dean demanded money in exchange for signing the adoption papers. He said he wouldn't relinquish his rights otherwise."

"He can't do that, can he?"

"No, he can't. It's illegal on several counts. He can't profit from an adoption, and he can't demand money in exchange for his cooperation. That's extortion."

She had never seen anyone who looked as hangdog as Richard did. Suddenly, she thought she understood. "You had Dean arrested, didn't you?"

"I'm an officer of the court. He was breaking the law. I had no choice."

"Oh, no."

"I hope you aren't worried about him. I doubt if he's still in jail. I understand from Chris that he was yelling for his lawyer all the way in."

"Of course I'm not worried about Dean. He's been in jail before. I can't believe I once thought that made him romantic. I'm upset because I brought more suffering to my father, more worry to my mother and more trouble for you."

"Dean caused the problems, not you."

"That's a pretty fine line, Counselor. If I hadn't hooked up with Dean, a lot of misery could have been avoided."

Richard pulled his chair closer and took her hand between his. "The past can't be changed. We have to look to the future. Your future and your baby's future."

"You're right. I won't wallow in self-pity. Once Dean hears that I'm keeping the baby, he'll take off again."

"Melissa, Dean can make trouble for you and for your baby for years and years."

"What do you mean?"

"He's the child's father. He has the exact same rights that you have. If he wants, he can take the baby away and you won't have a legal leg to stand on."

"You can't be serious?"

"I'm dead serious. I've seen it time and again. But we have another option."

"What option?"

"Hear me out before you say anything. In this state, when a woman marries, her husband is the presumed father under the law. It makes no difference who the child's biological father is, her husband is the legal father. Do you understand that?"

"Sort of."

"What I'm trying to say is that if you were to get married, your husband would be the baby's father. Now, Dean might be able to pursue a lengthy court battle to gain legal custody, but I believe that is unlikely."

"Richard, you're not suggesting what I think you're suggesting, are you?"

"I'm sorry, sweetheart. I know this isn't the way a woman wants a man to propose, but Melissa, you must know that I care about you deeply. I can be a husband to you and a father to your child. I can keep both of you safe. Give me the chance. Give me the honor. Will you marry me?"

Chapter Fifteen

Melissa stared at Richard, hardly believing that she had heard him correctly. Had he really just proposed? Was he kidding? Her heart leaped into triple time. Excitement danced along her nerve endings. She looked into his eyes, trying to read the emotion there, then blurted out the first thing that came to mind. "You can't be serious, can you?"

He met her gaze without flinching. "I've never been more serious in my life."

The realization of what he was asking hit her. "I don't know what to say."

"'Yes' would be a good answer."

Oh, how she wanted to shout the word. If only she could. It would be so easy to say yes, to put her future and her baby's future into his capable hands. He cared deeply for her. But that wasn't the same as love.

Her happiness fell as quickly as it had risen, leaving a hollow emptiness that might never be filled.

She reached out and laid her fingers on his cheek.

"That is the most gallant and selfless thing anyone has ever done for me."

"I'm not trying to be gallant."

"Yes, you are. Believe me when I say it is a tempting offer."

What an understatement. She looked down and began to smooth the edges of the sheet. He would shoulder all her troubles if she let him. It was a marvelous offer, if only he had said the words she longed to hear.

She loved him, but he didn't love her. That he was willing to give up finding his soul mate and settle for taking care of one unworthy woman and a child that wasn't his spoke volumes about the kind of man he truly was. That she was able to refuse his offer said something about the woman he had helped her to become.

He sat back. "You don't have to give me an answer tonight. I know my timing is lousy."

"Richard, you are a fine man. I think if you had asked me two days ago, I might have said yes."

Disappointment overshadowed the hope in his eyes. "But not now?"

Her next words almost broke her heart. "I won't let you make such a sacrifice for us."

"I'm not making a sacrifice."

"Even if you don't see it that way, I always would. That isn't fair to either of us."

"I'm going about this all wrong. Please reconsider, or at least take some time to think about it. Think about what this would mean for the baby."

"Thinking about it won't change my mind. I know you are doing this to protect me, but I don't need protection. I'll deal with Dean on my own terms. When I found the courage to tell my father that I'm keeping my baby, something changed for me. I know now that I can fight for her. I'm determined to make a life for the two of us. I understand that you want to help and I love you for that, but I'm asking you as a friend, a dear friend, let me make my own choices. Let me fight my own battles. Have faith in me."

"I do. You know that."

"Thank you. Now, I think I'd like to try and sleep for a little while." In a minute, she would start crying, and she didn't want him to see that.

He rose and shoved his hands in his pockets. "Of course. If there is anything you need, just call out."

"I will."

When he walked out the door, Melissa lay down and pulled the pillow to her face to muffle the sound of her sobs.

Richard walked down the hall and into the family room. He could hear Angela in the kitchen, but he didn't want company. He couldn't face anyone at this moment. Instead, he let himself out through the French doors that led to the covered patio.

The cool night air brushed his hot cheeks as he leaned against the smooth wooden post. The sounds of the night were settling over the neighborhood. Crickets chirped in the bushes, the breeze rustled the turning leaves. The hum of traffic was only sporadic now. Somewhere a car horn honked. They were such mundane sounds. There was nothing to indicate that this night was any different from a hundred other nights except the tightness in his throat.

She had said no. He had botched the whole thing. The

great attorney had messed up the most important argument of his life. She loved him like a dear friend. How inane that sounded.

No, he chided himself, Melissa's friendship was a great gift. Because she did not have more to offer him didn't mean he should value that friendship any less.

He walked out into the yard, away from the light and any prying eyes that might see him. There was a small bench at the end of the garden and he dropped onto the cold stone, putting his head in his hands as he tried to figure out what to do next.

"Lord, help me. I thought this was the right thing. I thought this was what You wanted from me. What do I do now?"

What was there to do? Nothing. She said no. She wanted to make a life for herself and for her baby. Her brave words showed exactly the kind of courage he always suspected she possessed. He would have to respect her wishes.

If he could just find a way to live with that.

The next morning, Melissa ventured out of her room reluctantly. She wasn't sure if she could face Richard without blurting out that she loved him or bursting into tears because he didn't love her.

She certainly hadn't gotten much sleep. As if a broken heart wasn't enough to keep her awake, her wrist ached all through the night. At least Heather's phone call had relieved her of one worry. Their father was stable, for now.

Settling herself at the kitchen table, Melissa accepted a cup of tea from Angela. She blew on the hot brew and tried to sound casual. "Is Richard up?"

"He left about half an hour ago. He said he had a busy day planned and that he would be late tonight. Did you need to speak to him?"

Melissa shook her head, then took a sip of her tea. At least she wasn't going to have to face him, yet. "Angela, can I ask you a favor?"

"Certainly."

"I want to apply for the work study program at the university. Can you bring me the forms?"

Angela's eyes widened. "Does this mean you're keeping the baby?"

"Yes, and I need a better job if I'm going to support both of us. The only way I can do that is to go back and finish school."

Throwing her arms around Melissa, Angela gave her a quick hug. "I'm so happy for you and so proud of you. Wait until the girls hear this. They're going to be as excited as I am. Of course I'll bring you the forms, and I'll talk to my friend who is looking for a research assistant. Girl, we are going to have you hitting the books in no time."

"You mean next semester. It's too late to enroll for this one."

"I'm not sure of the cutoff date, but I really want you to meet Barbara Haggerty. I think the two of you have a lot in common, especially your interest in women writers."

Melissa tried not to get her hopes up. "If she really needs an assistant, she isn't going to be able to wait until next semester. I see how heavy your workload is. Besides, I know I can't get a work study job unless I'm already enrolled as a student."

Angela looked crestfallen. "True, but I'll ask Barbara

to meet with you, anyway. She might be able to work something out."

After Richard's sister left, Melissa managed to get both girls out the door for school before she finally had a moment to call her mother. Nora answered on the second ring.

"Hi, Mom."

"Hello, darling. How are you?"

"I'm fine. Both of us are fine. How's Dad this morning?"

"Complaining about the food."

"That's a good sign."

"A very good sign."

"What does Dr. Strickland say?"

"He told us your father had a mild heart attack. The heart cath last night showed a small area of blockage in one of his coronary arteries. They opened it with a balloon angioplasty, but he's going to be monitored closely for at least another two weeks. The doctor is concerned that the antifungal medications your father is taking may complicate his recovery."

"Then Dad won't be home for Thanksgiving?"

"No. We are all very disappointed, but having him well is more important than having him home."

"Give him my love, will you? And tell him I'm sorry…about everything, especially about Dean's behavior."

"Honey, that wasn't your fault. You mustn't blame yourself."

"I don't. Dean can take credit for his own despicable behavior. I'm just sorry I gave him a reason to subject Dad to it."

After hanging up, Melissa dressed and went in to work. Ed Bradshaw was waiting by her desk when she arrived.

"Melissa, I've been looking over the information you gathered on Lettie McNeil. I'm impressed with what you have."

"Thank you."

"I want you to go ahead with the research. When you have a story you think is ready to run, come see me."

"I know it will make a great story." A bubble of happiness pushed aside her somber thoughts. He liked her idea.

He motioned toward her stomach. "Are you feeling okay? I heard about your accident."

"I sprained my wrist, but otherwise I'm fine."

"That's good. Well, don't just stand there. Croft in advertising needs a hand. We've got a paper to run. It's not going to print itself."

"Yes, sir." He sounded just like her father. She didn't salute, but she thought about it.

Over the next two days, Melissa kept busy at the paper and worked in her spare time on her project. Of Richard, she saw very little. She was almost certain that his workload hadn't expanded to the extent that he needed to be gone from the house from early in the morning until long after dark every night. He was avoiding her and she didn't know how to repair their friendship.

Angela and Dave's home was almost finished. In a few weeks they would be moving out of Richard's home. She would have to leave, too. She had put off looking for a place of her own, but she couldn't put it off any longer. Armed with a copy of the paper, she spent one afternoon checking out apartments within her current budget range. The results were depressing, to say the least.

Her current job didn't provide enough hours or enough pay to let her find a decent place. Even what she had saved by living with Richard and his family was barely enough for a deposit and the first month's rent.

Of course, she could ask her brother for more hours or a pay raise, but that wouldn't be making it on her own. Once, she might have considered moving back home, but not after her confrontation with her father. He would see it as a sign of weakness, as proof she couldn't take care of herself or a baby. One thing she *had* learned was that if people treated you as powerless, you began to see yourself that way and to act that way. No, going home wasn't an option.

She needed a second job if she was going to get ahead before the baby came.

On Friday, the week before Thanksgiving, she took her enrollment forms and the work-study application to the university. Angela had set up an appointment for her with Professor Haggerty. Outside the Women's Studies department, Melissa drew a deep breath before going in. Her fragile stab at independence was on the line. Getting a second job and getting into school were equally important.

"One small step at a time," she whispered under her breath, then she knocked on the door.

A woman's voice bade her enter. Inside, she was pleasantly surprised by the office. All the walls were covered with beautiful black-and-white portraits of women. Old women, young women, a few famous faces and some that were simply stunning in the strength of character gazing out from the photographs.

"I always love it when my office takes a young person's breath away."

A woman in her late fifties rose from behind a narrow desk in front of the windows. Dressed in a black jacket with wide white trim and a short black skirt, she looked as if she could have stepped down from one of the frames. She came forward and held out her hand. "I'm Barbara Haggerty. You must be Melissa Hamilton."

"I'm pleased to meet you, Professor. Thank you for seeing me."

"My pleasure. Please have a seat." She indicated a narrow sofa against the wall. "I've met your mother on several occasions. She is a supporter of Women's Studies at this university."

Melissa sat down. "That doesn't surprise me. My mother is a strong woman."

The professor returned to her chair behind her desk. She tipped her head to one side. "Like mother, like daughter?"

"I only hope that may be true."

Leaning back in her chair, Professor Haggerty steepled her fingers together and regarded Melissa with a slight frown. "Tell me, why does the daughter of Wallace Hamilton need a place in our work study program? Frankly, I thought the Hamiltons were the last family in this town to need financial assistance."

Melissa's hopes sank.

Chapter Sixteen

Melissa let herself into the quiet house. She hung her gray overcoat and scarf in the hall closet then carried her purse and books down the hall to her room. She breathed a sigh of pure relief as she kicked off her shoes and slipped her puffy feet into a pair of fluffy blue slippers.

Flopping onto the bed, she closed her eyes and reveled in a moment of quiet bliss. Until her stomach growled. She tried ignoring it without success.

"I can't believe I'm hungry again." But she was.

Sitting up, she stared at her bedroom door. There would be ice cream in the freezer. Or peanut butter and crackers in the cabinet. Her stomach rumbled a third time. She patted it and smiled.

"Okay, I get it, you want to be fed. I'm tired, but I guess I can make it as far as the kitchen."

Leaving her room, she walked down the hall, pausing to look into Richard's study. He wasn't in. Was he working late again or simply avoiding her?

She went on to the kitchen and stopped short inside

the doorway. Richard was making himself a sandwich. He looked up and their eyes met across the room. He looked tired. As tired as she felt. An awkward silence stretched between them.

No one had told her the proper etiquette for the first meeting with a man after she had refused his marriage proposal. What should she say? What was he thinking?

The best thing, she decided, was to act as if nothing were wrong instead of standing here as though her feet were nailed to the floor. "Where is everyone?" she asked.

"Angela is working late. Dave and the girls are outside putting together a new birdhouse. Their old one was accidentally knocked down and broken by the fire department when they were running hoses between the house and the street. Would you care for something to eat?"

"What are you having?"

"A grilled eggplant sandwich."

"Yuck." She pulled open the freezer and took out a pint of mint chocolate chip ice cream.

Richard smiled at the face she made. Did she have any idea how endearing she looked? "Eggplant is good for you."

"I'll take your word for it. Is there any peanut butter?"

"Sure. Do you want white bread or wheat?" Since she hadn't brought up the subject of his rejected proposal, he wouldn't, either.

She rummaged in the drawer for the ice cream scoop and ladled two large dips into a bowl. "No bread, just the peanut butter, thanks."

He watched as she spread a generous glob of it over her ice cream. "Talk about yuck. Are you going to eat that?"

"Yes, if there's any chocolate syrup."

"On the fridge door, second shelf. Do you usually eat peanut butter on your mint ice cream?"

"I've never tried it. It just sounds good. I hope I don't keep this up. I've got three more months to go. At this rate, I'll look like a blimp." She opened the refrigerator and pulled out the chocolate.

"You need to gain some weight."

She frowned at him over the open door. "You think I'm too skinny?"

Her defensive tone surprised him. "No, you're definitely not skinny."

She slammed the fridge shut. "So you think I'm fat, but not fat enough?" she demanded.

He opened his mouth, then closed it again and leveled his gaze at her. "I'm not sure how we got into this conversation, but I'm taking the fifth."

"Don't play counselor with me. You said I need to gain weight."

"What I meant was, all pregnant women need to gain a certain number of pounds in order to have a healthy baby."

"Oh."

"Am I okay now, or do I need to hide the kitchen knives?"

"I'm not sure. Let me think about it."

"While you're thinking, can I eat?"

"Yes." She moved toward the table with her bowl and he joined her.

"Angela told me you are going back to school."

She grinned. "I am, in the university's new program for single parents. I met with Angela's friend, Professor Haggarty."

"And she offered you a job?"

"At first she didn't think a Hamilton needed financial help."

"What made her change her mind?"

"I told her about my situation. I was up-front about the fact that I'm doing this without any help from my father."

"Did she think that was strange?"

"Not really. She said that she and her own father once shared vastly different opinions on her place in society. She seemed to understand that I want to be able to do this on my own. I was afraid I couldn't get into the program this late in the semester, but Professor Haggerty told me about their adult education classes. They have one class that is only on Saturday evenings for six weeks and it doesn't start until next weekend. I'm enrolled and I have a second job as her research assistant starting after Thanksgiving."

"That's great, but can you manage two jobs?"

"I have to keep my job at the paper because I need the insurance. The research I can do on weekends and in the evenings. I think it will work out." She took a bite of her ice cream.

"Things seem to be coming together for you." Letting go of his need to protect her was much harder than he expected.

"With a lot of help from you and your family. I don't think I will ever be able to thank you enough."

He took a bite of his sandwich to keep from repeating his proposal. How was he going to let this woman slip out of his life? How could he bear watching from the sidelines as she raised her daughter? He had been wrestling with the same questions for days. He still had no answers.

*Lord, I need Your wisdom now more than ever. Help
me do what is best for them.*

She stabbed her spoon into the concoction in her bowl
and stirred it. "All that's left is for me to find a place to live."

"Any ideas?"

"I've been looking at a few apartments. I'm trying not
to be picky, but what I can get on my salary isn't much."

"I have a few friends in the real estate business. I'll
make some inquiries, if that's okay with you?"

She studied her bowl, then looked at him. "As long
as you promise that you won't use any undue influence
on my behalf."

"You mean I can't do any arm-twisting?"

A grin tugged at the corner of her mouth. "No."

"No death threats?"

Her grin widened, as he had hoped. "Definitely, no
death threats."

"All right, no undue influence on your behalf. I
promise."

"Good."

Gazing into her smiling eyes, Richard knew he
couldn't give her up. She held a place firmly entrenched
in his heart. She wasn't indifferent to him, he was sure of
that. He would give her the space and the time she needed
to prove to herself, and to her family, that she could
manage on her own. He would bide his time and wait until
after the baby came. He would be her friend, and he would
pray that her feelings for him would grow into love.

"What are your plans for this weekend?" he asked,
trying to sound casual.

"On Saturday morning I'm going apartment hunting.
That is, if I can borrow your car for a few hours."

"Certainly. Anytime."

"Thanks. In the afternoon, Lettie has found a few more letters for me to look at." She looked down at her bowl and stirred the contents. He had the odd feeling that she was holding something back.

"What about Sunday?" he asked.

She looked up and met his gaze. A serene expression settled over her face. "On Sunday, I was hoping to go to church with you and your family."

Joy for her spread through his heart. That she was able to seek the Lord's presence meant more than he could express. He reached across the table and took her hand. "We would be honored to have you join us."

"Thanks, Richard. I knew you'd be happy."

To his dismay, she pulled her hand away and wouldn't meet his eyes.

The following morning, Melissa crossed off the third apartment on her list. She had only one more to see. The address was near the college, but it was apparently a house, not an apartment building. Holding out little hope, she drove toward the campus and turned onto a quiet street a few blocks south of the university.

She almost drove past it. Set back from the street was a small, narrow cottage painted bright yellow with white trim. She turned into the drive that ran past the house to a small detached garage. The whole property had a well-kept air. She allowed her hopes to rise. The rent was within her budget and this was certainly the best place she had seen so far. Now, if the inside looked as good as the outside.

An elderly woman appeared in the doorway of the

house next door. Melissa waved as she stepped out of the car. "I called about seeing your rental."

"Yes. Let me get the key." A few minutes later she was unlocking the door. "My last renter moved out after ten years. I was sure sorry to see her and her little girl go."

Inside, Melissa was pleasantly surprised by the open floor plan. The living room was divided from the dining room by twin square columns flanked by low, glass-fronted bookshelves. The dining room was small, but felt larger because of a wide bay window that jutted out and let the light pour into the room.

Following her host through a tiny but functional kitchen and down the hall, Melissa peeked into the bathroom. The green-and-white tile was vintage 1930s but everything looked in good shape. It was, however, the second bedroom at the end of the hall that truly won her heart. It was painted a deep rose with a white trim. The single window was deep set with a window seat covered in needlepoint upholstery depicting entwined hearts. "This will make a great nursery."

The landlady nodded. "I couldn't believe it when I got your call. Today is the first day my ad was in the paper. I surely thought I'd have a harder time renting this little place."

After having looked at quite a few inferior places, Melissa knew she had been fortunate to get here before anyone else, or blessed. Perhaps the Lord was looking out for her, after all.

Turning to the woman, Melissa grinned and said, "I'll take it."

After signing the papers and handing over a deposit, Melissa headed to Lettie's home. It wasn't long before she was once again engrossed in reading letters that were decades old.

"These are fabulous. I never knew people wrote such wonderful letters to each other."

Lettie, crocheting in a chair by the window, smiled. "You forget, not many folks had telephones back then. The country was still suffering the effects of the Depression. Visiting folks in another town was sometimes difficult. Writing came easily for us the way computers seem to come easily to this new generation."

"I guess that's true. May I have a few of these to make photocopies? I'll take care to see the originals aren't damaged or lost."

"Of course, dear."

Melissa noticed the balls of pink and white yarn spooling into Lettie's lap. "What are you working on?"

She held up a square with delicate pink and white fan shapes alternating across the width. "It's a baby blanket for you."

Tilting her head to one side, Melissa asked, "How did you know I'm keeping my baby?"

"I saw how happy you looked the minute you walked through the door."

Melissa cocked one eyebrow. "But you were working on that before I came in."

"Was I? I guess that's true. You didn't expect those girls of Angela's to keep it a secret, did you?"

"I guess not. They are really excited about getting to see the baby."

"Are you?"

Melissa grinned. "I'm really excited, too."

Lettie laid her needle and yarn aside. "Good. I've

got something that I'd like you to have. Mind you, it's only a loan, but I'd love for you to use it. I was going to wait till later, but I'm just busting to see what you think of it."

"What is it?"

Rising, Lettie hurried across the room. Melissa watched her in puzzlement. At the door to the hallway, Lettie looked back. "Come on. I can't carry it out here."

Melissa rose and followed her, curiosity burning a hole in her mind. What on earth could Lettie want to loan her that was too big to be moved?

At the second doorway in the hall, Lettie spun around, her hands clasped in front of her, looking exactly like Lauren did when she had something exciting to share. "Close your eyes," she commanded.

"Miss Lettie, is that really necessary?"

"Close your eyes and don't talk back to your elders."

"Yes, ma'am." Taking a deep breath, Melissa did as instructed.

She heard the sound of the door being opened and then she felt Lettie take her elbow. "Two steps forward."

Searching with her other hand for the doorjamb, Melissa located it and stepped through.

"Open your eyes, honey."

Melissa did and her breath caught in her throat. In the middle of the room sat an antique cradle.

The walnut headboard and footboard were both carved with an elaborate seashell design between panels of burled wood. Tall carved finials rose from each corner. The sides were rows of open walnut slats turned into elongated figure eights. Somehow the whole piece managed to seem massive and yet dainty at the same time. Stepping forward, she touched the side and the cradle rocked gently. "This is beautiful."

"It belonged to my grandmother. It's called an Eastlake Victorian cradle. I never had children of my own to rock in it, but Richard and Angela slept in it, as did their daddy and both of Angela's girls."

Melissa's delight quickly changed to consternation. "Lettie, this is a family heirloom. I can't use it."

"'Course you can. It's mine and I say who gets to put their babies in it."

Melissa threw her arms around the slender little woman. "You are so wonderful to me. How can I ever thank you?"

"I'll think of something, never you fear."

Stepping back, Melissa wiped at the moisture forming in the corners of her eyes. "I'm sure you will."

"For starters, you can come to church with me tomorrow."

Melissa forced her face into a frown. "Oh, I can't."

Fisting her hands on her hips, Lettie fixed her with an unblinking stare. "It's high time you went back to church, young lady. No baby that sleeps in the Corbet family crib is going to be brought up as a heathen."

Melissa couldn't keep her smile hidden. "I only meant I already agreed to go with someone else."

"With your mother?"

"No, I'm going with Richard and his family."

Lettie laughed. "Honey, that means you're coming with me, too. I told you I don't drive much. Richard or Angela always pick me up." A speculative gleam flashed in Lettie's eyes. "So my boy is taking you to church, is he? Fancy that."

Melissa's merriment faded. Lettie had no idea that Richard had proposed and that she had turned him down. "Miss Lettie, Richard and I are friends. You have to stop thinking that there's something more between us."

"Pshaw. I have a right to think anything I want. It's a free country."

"I just don't want you getting your hopes up."

"My hopes are exactly where they belong. I've never seen two people so bent on being friendly when it's as plain as day that they can't keep their eyes off each other. Now, you tell me I'm wrong about that."

"I think you're reading too much into what you see."

"All right. I'll stop nagging you and Richard, but I'm not going to stop hoping. You two would make a fine pair."

Lettie's words ran through Melissa's mind as she drove through town later that evening. If she had accepted Richard's offer, they wouldn't be a pair for long. Soon there would be a baby to make three. Dean's baby. Many a marriage where the couples started out in love with each other didn't survive the difficulties of raising children. And to raise another man's child, that was asking a lot. Even for as fine a man as Richard. She had done the right thing by turning him down. If only she could stop dreaming about living her life by his side.

Passing through the outskirts of Nashville, she pulled into the parking lot of a modestly popular nightclub. The lot was empty except for two white vans parked near the side doors. She watched as three men came out of the club and lifted a large set of speakers from one of the vans. She recognized all three of them, but the man she was here to see wasn't among them.

Melissa stepped out of the car and walked toward the nightclub, trying to ignore the rush of apprehension pouring through her veins.

Chapter Seventeen

As Melissa stepped through the large, metal side doors of the club, she paused to let her eyes adjust to the dim light. The room was packed with an assortment of mismatched tables and chairs around a small dance floor that looked as if it hadn't had a good cleaning in years. Mirrors on the walls reflected the shabby scene, but did nothing to lighten the place's dark mood. The nauseating smell of stale cigarette smoke permeated the air.

How could she ever have imagined that a life in places like this night after night was what she had wanted?

The band was already on the low stage. Dean stood near the microphone testing the sound of his guitar while the other two band members were hooking up the amplifiers. She walked to the foot of the platform and waited until Dean noticed her. She knew he had seen her by the sour note he struck.

"What do *you* want?" he demanded in a grim tone.

"Could I talk to you for a few minutes?"

"Anything you need to say can be said to my lawyer."

"This is about us. Not about anything else that happened."

"Your papa's watchdog attorney might see it differently."

"Please, Dean. I'm only asking for a few minutes."

He glared at her, but she didn't back down. This was important and it needed to be settled before she could move on.

"All right. I'll give you five minutes." He slipped the strap of his guitar off over his head and laid the instrument on the floor, then he hopped off the stage. He flipped his long hair back, then pulled a pack of cigarettes from his pocket and lit one. "Say what you've got to say."

"Outside." She wasn't about to discuss their personal life in front of the other band members. She turned on her heels and walked out, not knowing if he would follow.

He did. She stopped beside the closest van and faced him. "I came to tell you that I'm keeping the baby."

"Oh, so now you're gonna sue to make me pay child support?"

"I'm not asking for child support. As far as I'm concerned, since you've never wanted this baby, I see no reason to include you in my child's life unless you want it. Do you?"

He threw his cigarette down and ground it under his boot heel. "I should say yes just to see you squirm."

"I won't squirm. If I really believed that you wanted to be a part of our child's life, I would let you. But I know that isn't the case. I won't let you use her as a weapon to hurt me or my family. If you try, I'll take you to court and prove to everyone you are an unfit parent. The fact that you abandoned me in Detroit will be easy to prove, as will your drug habit. Don't forget, I know all about that, but I'm sure your manager doesn't. You'll gain nothing by fighting me except a stack of bills for legal fees."

He took a menacing step toward her. "If I hadn't thought I could get a hold of your old man's money, I never would have hooked up with you."

"It was a mistake for both of us. After the baby is born, I'll have papers sent to you so that you can relinquish your parental rights. I don't want anything from you, except that. I think it will be best if we never see each other again."

He crossed his arms and leaned one shoulder against the van. "Have your daddy drop the charges against me and I'll consider relinquishing my rights."

"My daughter isn't a bargaining chip. You will have to pay for your own mistakes. Sign or don't sign, it's up to you. But know this, you won't have a part in this baby's life. I'm not your pawn, Dean. I've learned a little about standing up for myself in the past month."

"Who's been teaching you? Daddy's attorney?"

"Among other people, yes. I'm getting my life back on track. I'm not getting a penny of Daddy's money so you don't have to feel bad thinking the rich girl got away."

"Right. Like I believe that."

"I feel sorry for you, Dean. You have talent, but you are always looking for the quick fix, the easy road. There isn't one. I also came to tell you that I forgive you for the way you treated me. Have a nice life, Dean. I'll pray for you."

She turned and began walking to the car. Her knees were shaking so badly she wondered if she could make it.

"Pray for yourself, Melissa," he shouted after her. "You're the one who needs it, not me."

She stopped and looked back. "I do need it. Say one for me and for your daughter if you ever feel like praying. I hope someday you will."

Sunday morning the sun was shining brightly as Melissa walked with Richard toward the Northside Community Church. Located on a gentle rise, the white brick building overlooked an expanse of shady lawn that rolled away to the tree-lined edge of the river below. Looking up, she saw the steeple silhouetted against a flawless blue sky. She mounted the broad steps leading up to a columned portico with a growing sense of happiness. It seemed so right to be here.

Inside the building, a deep awareness of real peace settled over her as she made her way down the central aisle. Overhead, the vaulted ceiling, spanned by heavy oak beams, gave the building a feeling of expansiveness. Brilliant colors spilled into the space from tall, arched, stained-glass windows on either side. In a pew near the front, Melissa saw her mother sitting with Amy and Heather.

As Richard's family filed into a pew on the opposite side, Melissa touched Richard's arm. "Thank you for bringing me here," she said quietly, "but I think I'll sit with Mom."

Richard smiled, his eyes filled with understanding. "I think that's a great idea."

Walking the rest of the way alone, Melissa stopped beside her mother. "Is there room here for one more?"

Nora stood and threw her arms around Melissa. "Always," she whispered, her voice choked with emotion. "There is always, always room for one more in God's house."

"I'm learning that."

As they took their seats, both Heather and Amy reached out to squeeze Melissa's hand in welcome. A moment later, the congregation rose as the minister approached the pulpit. Together, the voices of the people were lifted up in song. With a hymnal in hand, Melissa sneaked a peek back at Richard. He was singing, but his eyes were on her.

Samantha stood beside him, singing in a beautiful alto that carried each note clear and true. She caught Melissa's eye and smiled. Melissa gave her a thumbs-up sign. If the choir director was listening, he certainly would be blown away by the improvement in the girl's voice.

Following the opening song, the congregation sat down and Reverend Abernathy began his sermon. He spoke sincerely and eloquently about the meaning of Thanksgiving. As Melissa listened, she silently listed all the things she was grateful for in her life. So many of her troubles that had once seemed like unbearable burdens were bearable now that she had faced up to them and stopped running away.

God had opened her heart to the good in people. People like her mother and her brothers and sisters. People like Richard, who cared about others and sought to help. Closing her eyes, she gave thanks for the people she loved, for her baby, and her family, and for the man seated a few rows back. A man she loved deeply.

As she prayed, her father's face came to mind. He was the one part of her life that she hadn't made peace with. Perhaps she never would, but she knew she had to try.

Later, when the service was over, she spoke to her

mother as they were leaving the church. "Mom, how is Dad?"

"Better I think. Dr. Strickland seems quite hopeful that your father will make a full recovery."

"Do you think it would be all right if I went to see him?"

"Of course it would. You don't have to ask that."

"It's just that I don't want to upset him."

"He's worried about you. Seeing you would do him a world of good."

"Do you really think so?"

"Darling, I know so."

"All right. I'll go. I'll go this afternoon. That is, if you're sure?"

"I'll drive you myself."

Melissa chewed her lower lip, then blurted out, "No offence, Mom, but I think I'd rather see him alone."

"I understand. I'll drop you off and you can call me when you're ready to leave. How's that?"

"That would be fine. Could we go now, before I lose my nerve?"

"Certainly, and don't worry about your nerve. I suspect you will find in time that you have inherited your father's nerves of steel."

The drive to the hospital didn't take long with the light Sunday traffic. Melissa stood in the parking lot and watched her mother drive away with a sinking sense of dread. Why on earth had she insisted on seeing her father alone?

Because with her mother present, both Melissa and Wallace would have maintained a polite demeanor and nothing important would have been said.

She stared up at the austere building, waiting for her

fear to creep out and choke her, but nothing happened. Jenny's death had been tragic, but Jenny was at peace. Melissa knew it in her heart. Squaring her shoulders, she walked through the doors.

Outside her father's room, she paused only a second. If she waited, she might lose her resolve. She tapped lightly and opened the door before he answered.

Wallace was sitting up in bed with a Bible in his hands. A set of gray wires protruded from inside his navy-blue pajama top. They led to a cardiac monitor over the bed where his heartbeat was displayed by a green, bouncing line. A tray of food had been pushed to one side. It looked as if he had eaten very little.

He laid his book aside. "Melissa, are you all right?"

"I'm fine, Daddy."

"Come in, sit down."

"How are you feeling?" She approached the foot of his bed.

"I'd be better if they'd let me out of this place."

She nodded toward the tray. "They aren't going to let you go if you don't eat better than that."

"The food here is terrible. Everything tastes like paste."

"Mom told me you'd been complaining about the meals."

"I miss her cooking. Are you sure you're all right?"

"Yes, I'm sure."

"And the baby?"

Melissa patted her stomach. "Your granddaughter is fine."

"My granddaughter. That is going to take some getting used to."

"About the other day, Dad—"

"I'm so sorry," he interrupted. "When they told me about your fall I thought…I thought you might never want to see me again. I shouldn't have spoken to you like that."

"When Richard told me what Dean tried to do, I thought you might never want to see *me* again."

"It looks like we were both wrong," he said with a wry smile.

"I'm sorry for so many things, Daddy…I don't even know where to start."

"Me, too." He held out his arms and Melissa rushed to him. He held her close and patted her back as she broke down and cried for all the misery and misunderstanding that had kept them apart for so long.

"Don't cry so. You'll make yourself sick."

When she was able to regain a measure of composure, Melissa sat back on the side of the bed and wiped her face. "I don't think these tears…will make me sick. I think…these tears are going to make me better. Don't worry, I cry all the time. I think it's the pregnancy."

Wallace wiped his eyes with the back of his sleeve. "Your mother was that way when she was pregnant with the twins. I tiptoed around for months trying not to upset her."

"Did it work?"

"No, she cried at every little thing. Once, I found her at the window crying because it was such a beautiful, sunny day. Two days later, she's crying because the sound of the rain made her happy. The next day she was crying because she looked too fat in her favorite dress. That was a long nine months."

Melissa managed a weak smile. "I'm not quite that bad, but I have a few months to go."

"Are you sure keeping the baby is what you want? It isn't going to be easy." His doubts were evident in his face. A few days ago, his tone would have been enough to send her self-esteem plummeting.

Heavenly Father, give me the chance to prove to this man that I have changed.

She sat up straighter. "It *is* what I want. I know there will be tough times, but I have God and my family in my corner, so I'm going to be fine."

He reached out and touched her face. "You remind me of your mother."

"Daddy, I do believe that's the finest compliment I've ever received."

Richard drove Lettie home after the service. She was unusually quiet on the trip, but then, he wasn't much in the mood for conversation. Melissa had looked so happy today. He couldn't get her image out of his mind. The more he tried to get on with his life, the more he found himself thinking about her. Living in the same house with her and not being able to tell her how much he loved her was torture.

As he pulled up to the curb in front of his aunt's place, Lettie spoke at last. "What's eating you, Richard?"

"Nothing." He turned off the engine but didn't get out.

"Don't be fibbing to me. I can see you got something heavy on your mind. It's as plain as the nose on your face."

"That plain?"

"Reminds me of the way Melissa's been looking."

"I thought she looked happy today."

"Happy? I thought she looked downright beautiful."

"She is beautiful, inside as well as outside."

"Except when she's moping over you."

"What? No, you've got that all wrong. She isn't moping over me."

"Don't be contradicting your elders. If I say the girl is moping over you, she is."

"I'd like to think that's true, but I know better." He couldn't help the bitterness that crept into his voice.

"All right, I'll bite. How do you know it isn't true?"

"Because I asked Melissa to marry me and she said no."

Lettie stared at him openmouthed. "How could a man as smart as you mess up a proposal so badly?"

"I didn't mess it up."

"If that girl told you no, sugar, you messed up bad."

"Lettie, I'd really rather not talk about this."

"I can see why. I'd be embarrassed, too, if I made such a fool of myself."

"I didn't make a fool of myself. I asked her to marry me and she turned me down."

"Did you tell her how much you loved her? Did you mention that you couldn't live without her? Did you tell her you give thanks to God every day for bringing her and her baby into your life?"

"Not in so many words."

"I was right. You messed up."

"I can't believe I'm having this discussion with you."

"Who else you gonna tell?"

Who else, indeed? He gripped the top of the steering wheel. The need to share his disappointment was stronger than his need to hide his wounded pride. "I told her that I cared deeply for her. I said I wanted to protect her and be a father to her child. I even said that if she married me before the baby was born I would be considered the legal father and Dean Orton wouldn't be able to threaten her ever again."

"Oh my stars, you didn't say that?"

"What's wrong with wanting to protect her?"

"Sugar, a woman doesn't want a man listing all the reasons why it's a good idea to get hitched. A woman wants a man to say he loves her and life without her as his wife isn't worth living. She wants passion, not common sense. You ask her again. That gal is in love with you."

"She's had so many adjustments in her life, lately. I don't want to pressure her. I won't say anything until after the baby is born."

"Well, you're a good boy, Richard. I can see you have her best interests at heart. But you take my advice, don't wait too long. I don't see any sense in both of you being miserable for months when a little plain speaking and a kiss or two would make the world right as rain in no time."

Tuesday afternoon, Nora set a curtain rod into the brackets and adjusted the white eyelet ruffles until they hung to her satisfaction. She stepped down from the folding ladder and surveyed her work. "How does this look?"

"It looks great, Mom." Melissa, on her knees by the bookcases, added the last volume to the shelf and closed the glass-fronted door.

"This is a charming house." Nora, looking far younger than fifty-five in a pair of dark blue jeans and a lemon-yellow T-shirt, sank into the room's only chair, a worn green recliner that had seen better days.

"I was blessed to get it. All it needs now is some furniture." Her new living room was empty except for the chair and a half-dozen boxes taking up space along one wall. Melissa stood and dusted off her faded jeans. She let out a heartfelt sigh.

"Are you tired, dear?"

Melissa appreciated her mother's sympathy and her help. "After a busy day at work, packing and unpacking isn't as much fun as it should be."

"Why don't you take a rest? I can finish the curtains."

"No, I'm okay. Besides, take a rest on what? I don't even own a bed yet."

Nora glanced at her watch. "Your bed and dresser from the house should be here any minute. The movers said six-thirty."

As if on cue, someone knocked on the front door. "I'll get it," Nora said. Melissa didn't argue. She pressed her hands to the small of her aching back and stretched.

"Hello, Nora. Is Melissa here?"

Melissa's heart skipped a beat, then sped up at the sound of Richard's deep voice. She moved to stand beside her mother. He looked more handsome than ever in brown corduroy pants and a deep gold sweater with the sleeves pushed up past his elbows. The masculine scent of his cologne sent a skittering tingle of awareness racing along her nerve endings.

"Richard, what are you doing here?" Melissa heard the breathy catch in her own voice, but hoped he hadn't noticed.

"I come bearing gifts from Lettie." He indicated a large box beside him on the porch.

"You brought the cradle? Oh, how wonderful. Mom, wait until you see this."

"Where would you like it?" Richard asked.

"Through the kitchen and down the hall. The second door on the left is going to be the nursery."

"Through the kitchen and down the hall it is," he said. Grasping the edges of the box, he maneuvered it through the front door. Melissa waited until he had it inside, then she grabbed the other end.

"Don't lift that," he and Nora scolded at the same time.

Melissa threw her hands in the air. "All right. I won't lift it, but I'm not an invalid, I'm only pregnant."

Nora shooed her aside. "We can manage without you."

"I want to help. After all, this is my house."

"Your job is to look pretty and supervise," Richard stated.

Melissa knew she was blushing by the heat that rushed to her face. It was a simple, innocent comment. She shouldn't read more into it. Stepping aside, she let them wrestle the box through the house. It didn't take long for Richard and Nora to set the cradle up in the center of the nursery. Melissa parked herself on the window seat until they were finished.

"Richard, this is beautiful," Nora said, running her hand over the rich wood.

"It's been in Lettie's family for generations." He gave it a push and set it to rocking gently.

"What a wonderful tradition to pass on," Nora said.

Watching him, Melissa wondered how he felt about her baby using something that belonged to his family. If he had any objections, she knew he would never admit to them. "I'll take good care of it," she promised.

He smiled at her. "I never doubted that for a second. I'm glad Lettie thought of it. Cradles are made to hold babies. To see one sitting empty is a little sad."

"Speaking of traditions," Nora said, "One of the Hamilton traditions is to invite our friends to share dinner on Thanksgivings. I was hoping that you and your family would join us. Please don't say no, Richard. You've always been like part of the family to us."

She slipped her arm across Melissa's shoulder. "I have so much to be thankful for this year. Please say you will join us."

Melissa met his gaze and saw uncertainty in his eyes. Their relationship, while friendly, continued to be strained since she had refused his proposal. It was up to her to try and put him at ease. "I'd love it if you and your family would come, Richard. Please, say you will."

Chapter Eighteen

The morning of Thanksgiving dawned bright and clear. Melissa rose early; excitement had made it hard to sleep. She would be going home for the first time in months. Not with her head hung in shame, but with her head held high, proud of the changes she had made in her life. She took a moment to give thanks to God for showing her the way.

Armed with an index card written in Lettie's flowing handwriting, Melissa tackled a pecan pie. When she pulled it out of the oven an hour later, she knew she had succeeded in baking a pie that looked and smelled good. The real test would come when Richard tasted it.

The thought brought her up short. He wouldn't be the only one at dinner, but his opinion was the one that really mattered.

"You poor woman," she muttered. "In this day and age you are worried a man won't like your cooking. Get a grip."

It was good advice, but she was pretty sure she wasn't going to follow it. So much about Richard's life and likes were important to her. She worried about his health and the stress his job sometimes caused him. She wanted to hear about his day and tell him about hers. She wanted to be included in every part of his life. If only he had proposed because he loved her.

But he hadn't. He had proposed because he wanted to protect her and her baby. As noble as that was, it wasn't something to base a marriage on.

Later that morning, she stood on the porch outside her mother's front door, foil-covered pie in hand, and rang the bell. The heavy, leaded-glass-inlaid front door swung open revealing Vera Mae, the family's part-time housekeeper and dear friend. With her gray hair pulled back into a bun, a bright smile of welcome on her face and a sizable apron covering her best lavender dress, Vera Mae was as much a part of Melissa's childhood memories of her home as the wide staircase banister and her grandmother's grand piano in the little parlor.

"Miss Melissa, if you aren't a sight for sore eyes. Come here and give me a hug, baby girl. It's so good to have you home."

Before Melissa could comply, she was engulfed by Vera Mae's ample arms. She barely had time to keep the pie from getting squished between them.

"It's good to be home, Vera Mae. Happy Thanksgiving," she managed to whisper past the lump of emotion in her throat.

Vera Mae released Melissa and dabbed at her eyes with the corner of her large white apron. "The same to you, child. Come in. Most of the family is already here, except your brother, Jeremy. I do wish he would call your mother. She worries about him so."

"Where is she?"

"She's in the kitchen putting the finishing touches on the meal. You know how she is, she wants everything to be perfect for her children. What have you got there?" She pointed to the dish in Melissa's hands.

"My contribution to the feast. I baked a pie."

"I declare, will wonders never cease!"

"Vera Mae," Melissa declared in mock chagrin. "I cook a little. It's not rocket science."

"I'm sure it will be wonderful. I'll take it to the table."

Melissa followed her through the foyer and into the dining room where the antique oak table had been expanded for the occasion to accommodate the family and all the guests. The dark wood, set with her mother's best china, gleamed with loving care and the scent of lemon oil and furniture polish vied with the smell of turkey and sage drifting in from the kitchen.

Melissa's heart expanded with a wealth of emotions. Memories of happy times gathered around this table with the people she loved filled her mind. How sad that she had discarded it all out of bitterness and fear, and how wonderful was the Lord to bring her home again. Smiling, she joined the rest of her family gathered around the TV in the next room.

A series of moans issued from the men as she paused in the doorway. Since no one was looking in her direction, she was certain she wasn't the cause of the disgruntled sound. Chris was seated in the overstuffed chair with Felicity perched on the arm beside him. Heather and Amy sat on the sofa with Bryan and Ethan on either side of them. Tim and Dawn looked very cozy on the love seat opposite the sofa. Dave, leaning forward with his elbow propped on his knees, occupied a straight-backed chair at the end of the love seat, while Angela stood looking out the window. Through the French doors leading out onto the patio and the lawns, Melissa saw Dylan, Samantha and Lauren tossing a Frisbee back and forth.

Another groan rose from the men. "Can you believe that?" Chris shouted.

"Favorite football team not doing well?" Melissa asked.

Chris, closest to door, rose to his feet and gave her a quick hug. "They fumbled on the eight-yard line. Happy Thanksgiving, little sis."

"Same to you, and to all of you."

Hugs were exchanged all around, but the one person she wanted to see seemed to be missing. Where was Richard? Suddenly, Melissa was struck with a stab of self-pity. Everyone in the room had someone they loved at their side. Her sisters looked radiantly happy. Even her brothers looked happier and more carefree than she had ever seen them. Only she was the odd one out.

"I never did get into the football thing," she said after everyone returned to their seat. "I'm going to see if Mother needs any help in the kitchen."

"Mom, Miss Lettie and Vera Mae threw me out half an hour ago, but you can try," Amy offered.

"No need to go looking for me," Nora said from behind Melissa. "Dinner is ready. Hello, sweetie."

"Hi, Mom." Melissa kissed her cheek.

"About time. I'm starved," Chris said. Felicity gave him a playful smack on his shoulder.

"What?" he demanded. "I get grumpy when I'm hungry."

"You get grumpy when your team is losing."

"That, too. How is it that you know me so well?"

Felicity winked at Melissa. "I have my sources."

In the general bedlam of calling the children in, sending them to wash up and then finding places for everyone at the long table, Melissa ended up with Lauren on one side of her and Lettie on the other. It wasn't until she sat down that she realized she was directly across from Richard.

"Happy Thanksgiving, Melissa," he said over the growing hubbub of voices.

She knew she was blushing. Would he always have this effect on her? She smiled and hoped it didn't look as wistful as it felt. "Happy Thanksgiving, Richard. I didn't see you when I came in."

"I was outside with the kids."

She should have known. He loved spending time with kids. "You're going to make a wonderful father."

Melissa realized she had spoken the thought aloud when a startled look crossed his face.

"I mean, someday." She looked down at her plate. "When you find the right person."

Lettie leaned toward Melissa. "Maybe. If he isn't so dense that he lets her get away."

Richard scowled at Lettie but didn't say anything. Melissa felt compelled to defend him. "Richard isn't dense, Miss Lettie."

"Couldn't prove it by me," she stated.

Nora drew everyone's attention by tapping her spoon on the side of her glass. Quickly, the table grew quiet. She laid her spoon down and smiled. "I can't tell you how happy I am to have so many of my family and friends with me today. Wallace and I want to wish all of you the happiest of holidays. Even though he can't be here with us today, he wants you all to know that he is with you in spirit. And he especially wanted me to ask Vera Mae to smuggle some of her peach cobbler into the hospital tonight."

"I've already saved him a big ol' slice, Miss Nora."

Everyone laughed, including Nora. "Wonderful. Now, let us bow our heads and give thanks to the Lord for His bounty. I ask you to pray not only for Wallace, but also for Jeremy, who can't be with us today."

"Prayers for me won't be necessary, Mom."

They all turned in surprise to see Jeremy standing in the doorway. A moment of stunned silence followed.

Melissa saw at a glance that her oldest brother had changed in the past months. Gone was his casual, confident air. In its place she saw uncertainty in his piercing blue eyes and perhaps a touch of bitterness. He stood aloof and alone and her heart went out to him.

She glanced from Jeremy to Tim and saw that Tim was on his feet. She couldn't decipher the look on his face. She knew her brothers had parted on bad terms. Was there going to be another scene?

Tim left his place at the table and crossed the room to stand in front of Jeremy. He held out his hand. "I acted like a jerk. Can you forgive me?"

The expression on Jeremy's face softened. "I can— if you can forgive me for the way I've acted." He took his brother's hand and pulled him into a hug.

Melissa and the rest of her siblings left their places to join Tim in welcoming Jeremy home. Jeremy's face broke into a smile when Melissa reached him. He held her close and kissed the top of her head.

"The prodigal daughter has returned, I see," he said.

She grinned up at him. "Along with the prodigal son."

His smile faded. "Stepson."

"You'll always be my big brother. Nothing changes that."

"Thanks, kid." He leaned back. "You look different."

"Tell her she looks fat and you're a dead man," Richard told him as he stood at her side, extending his hand to Jeremy. "I'm glad you're back."

Jeremy shook Richard's hand as he glanced between the two of them. "What did I miss?"

"A lot," Melissa said. "I'll fill you in later. For now, I think Mom is waiting for you."

Nora stood near the head of the table, her hands clasped together over her heart, tears of joy sparkling in her eyes. Jeremy moved out of the circle of his siblings and walked toward her. He stopped a step away. "Can you forgive me, Mom?"

She reached out and took his face between her hands. "There is nothing to forgive. You're here and that's all that matters." She moved into his embrace and for a long moment, mother and son stood unmoving, holding each other close.

Richard watched Melissa wipe at the tears forming in her eyes. He offered her his handkerchief. She accepted it and sent him a grateful smile.

Jeremy turned to face the rest of the family, but kept his arm around his mother. "The one true thing I have learned in my time away is just how much this family means to me. I've missed you all. I couldn't imagine spending Thanksgiving anywhere else."

"We're glad you are here. What are your plans?" Nora asked, looking up with adoring eyes.

"I'm not sure."

Tim spoke up. "You can have any job you want at Hamilton Media. I mean that. Any job."

"Thanks, Tim, but I'm not sure what I want just yet."

Nora said, "It's enough that you are home. Please, everyone come back to the table. We don't want the turkey to get cold."

Richard took his place opposite Melissa and drank in the sight of her happiness. He was glad for her sake, and Nora's, that Jeremy was home, but he knew Jeremy and Wallace would still face difficult times. For Jeremy to learn so late in life that the man he loved wasn't his father must have been a painful blow.

Looking at Melissa, Richard decided her daughter would know from the start that she was the child of his heart, if not of his flesh and blood. After all, her mother was the woman who owned his heart. Somehow, he had to make Melissa believe that.

After Nora led the family in a beautiful blessing, the entire gathering quickly took on a festive quality. Heaping platters of turkey, corn bread dressing, black-eyed peas and other traditional foods were passed from one end of the table to the other and back again.

By the time the desserts made their way down the table, stories of previous Thanksgiving disasters and laughter filled the room. Richard helped himself to a generous slice of the pecan pie and passed it on. Melissa took a small slice of the pumpkin pie and kept glancing toward him. She seemed unusually interested in something on his plate. He made a quick check of his shirtfront to make sure he wasn't wearing a splotch of gravy. Seeing nothing, he cut into the pie and forked a bite into his mouth.

"How is it?" Melissa asked, sounding breathless and on edge.

"Great," he mumbled around his mouthful.

"Oh, good." She relaxed with a self-satisfied smile.

He swallowed his bite. "Lettie makes the best pecan pie in the country. You should try some."

Lettie, looking as smug as a cat with canary feathers sticking out of its mouth, said, "I didn't bring a pecan pie today."

"Really? This tastes every bit as good as yours." He forked another piece in his mouth.

Lettie turned to Melissa. "Didn't Vera Mae tell me that you brought this luscious, made-from-scratch pecan pie?"

Melissa nodded, looking pleased. "I'm glad it turned out okay."

Lettie propped her elbow on the table and set her chin on her hand. Smiling sweetly at Richard, she said, "I declare. It looks like this gal can make a pecan pie just as good as mine."

Richard wisely chose not to reply.

The conversation at the table soon turned to the upcoming weddings that were being planned. It was while Amy and Heather were telling Jeremy about shopping for wedding dresses that Richard happened to glance at Melissa. Her earlier happiness had faded. Now, she simply looked sad. She caught him looking and tried to smile, but she didn't fool him.

She excused herself with a word to Lettie and left the table. He watched her go, wondering what he could do to help. He would give anything to see her happy again. A sharp pain in his shin brought his attention back to his aunt.

"Go after her," Lettie said, motioning with her head.

He rubbed his smarting leg. "I don't think I can walk."

She leaned forward. "Go, or I'll kick the other one."

He wasn't sure which he dreaded more, Lettie's torture or having Melissa rebuff him again. No, that wasn't true. He was more afraid of having Melissa say no again than anything he had ever faced. He gathered his courage, rose from the table and followed Melissa into the adjoining room.

He found her standing by the window. She looked embarrassed, and adorable as she sniffed into his hankie.

She waved one hand. "I'm crying again. I can't help it."

"What's wrong, Lissa?" He moved to take her by the shoulders.

"Everyone is so happy." She sniffled again. "Everyone is planning weddings and making sheep eyes at the people they love."

"And that makes you cry?"

"Yes."

He pulled her close. "Why?"

She sobbed twice. "Be—be—because."

"Because you don't have someone making sheep eyes at you?"

She shook her head. "Don't be silly."

He put one finger under her chin. "I'm not sure how the sheep do it, but if you look up here you'll see someone who loves looking at you."

She turned her face away. "Don't."

The noise of the other room faded as he looked upon the woman he loved. "Don't what? Don't tell you that I love you beyond all reason? Don't tell you that the sun looks dim compared to the brightness of your smile? Don't tell you that I will never love another woman but you?"

"Yes."

"I have to tell you these things because they are true."

"You just want to rescue me."

"I thought that once, but more and more I see that you don't need rescuing."

She peeked at him from beneath her lashes. "You do?"

"I do. I see a strong woman finding her own path in life."

"I am."

"I noticed, but I desperately need to know something."

"What?" Her voice was so low he barely heard her.

"Can I share your path, please?"

She looked at him then, doubt clouding her beautiful eyes. "Do you mean it? Do you really love me?"

He took a step back and, holding on to both her hands, he dropped to one knee. "I love you, I love you, I love you!" he shouted at the top of his voice. "Will you marry me?"

The voices in the dinning room grew suddenly silent. "That a boy!" Lettie called out.

Melissa stared at Richard as her disbelief slowly gave way to joy so sharp she could hardly breathe. "I love you, too."

She heard the scrape of chairs from the other room and a second later, Lettie and Lauren were standing in the doorway. "Well, girl, what's your answer? Speak up," Lettie declared.

Richard stood, blocking her from the doorway that was quickly filling with interested family members. "Will you marry me?" he whispered, never taking his eyes off hers.

"Yes, I'll marry you," she whispered back.

"And may I share your chosen path?"

"Every step of the way."

"What did she say?" Lauren called out.

"Shall we keep them in suspense a little longer?" he asked with a grin only she could see.

"I think they've waited long enough." She leaned to the side and looked at the gallery forming in the doorway. "I said yes!"

Cheers broke out and her family rushed in. Lauren was the first to reach her. She threw her arms around Melissa's waist. "Now I'll have a cousin to play with."

"It's about time," Lettie said, smiling like a fool. "I was beginning to wonder if I'd live to see the day."

Tim and Chris pumped Richard's hand and slapped him on the back as Nora hugged Melissa.

"You look a little shell-shocked, Mom," Melissa said.

"I'm so happy for you, but I'm thinking—five weddings in a year. How am I going to do this?"

Vera Mae worked her way in to hug Melissa. "Never you mind about that, Miss Nora. You'll have lots of help."

Melissa accepted hugs and congratulations from Richard's family as well as her own. As her gaze swept around the room, she noticed Jeremy standing apart from the others. She crossed the room to stand beside him. Taking his arm, she said, "Let's go for a walk. We have a lot of catching up to do."

"I'll say."

She turned to face everyone in the room, but it was Richard who caught and held her gaze. "I can't thank you enough for the love and support you have all shown me in the past weeks. I once doubted that God cared about me. I see now how blind I was. He brought me back to my family and gave me someone special to love."

She glanced down and touched her stomach, then smiled at Richard. "Actually, He's given me two special someones to love."

"What?" Jeremy interjected, looking totally stunned.

She patted his arm and pulled him toward the door. "Boy, do we have a lot of catching up to do." At the doorway, she turned and blew a kiss to Richard.

He watched her go with a heart full of pride. She had grown into a beautiful and loving woman and she was going to share his life. He was overwhelmed with happiness.

"Did you kiss her?" Lettie demanded from beside him.

He looked heavenward. "No. Not yet."

"Richard, what am I going to do with you?"

"There was quite a crowd, if I recall. Not exactly the time and place for kissing."

She shoved him toward the entry. "Go after her, and when she is done talking to her brother you find some-place quiet and kiss that girl."

Grinning, he gave his aunt a quick kiss on her cheek. "Aunt Lettie, that's one order I'll be happy to follow." He winked, then sprinted for the door.

* * * * *

Dear Reader,

Writing *Prodigal Daughter* proved to be more difficult than I had dreamed and even more rewarding than I had dared hope.

Many years ago, my daughter gave me the news every mother of a teenage girl dreads to hear. She was pregnant. It was a very difficult time for my family. Ultimately, through prayer and God's grace, we became a stronger and more caring family because of it. Today, I can't imagine a world without my grandchildren. They have been God's greatest gift to me.

To write this story I had to put myself in the heroine's shoes. In trying to reach the emotions that all unwed mothers must face, I also had to put myself in my daughter's shoes. It wasn't easy trying to see what those uncertain days must have been like for her. It was a heart-wrenching journey for me, but one that was worth taking. I hope I have done justice to it here.

Blessings to all.

Patricia Davids

QUESTIONS FOR DISCUSSION

1. What was the nature of Melissa's relationship with her father? How did their relationship affect her?

2. Was Richard right to offer Melissa a place to live without asking her family first? Why or why not? What would you have done?

3. Many young women face unwed pregnancies each year. How do you think you would react to the news that your daughter or granddaughter was about to become an unwed mother?

4. What was the role of Aunt Lettie in Melissa's journey toward God? Has someone helped you in your journey in a similar way? Share a story about that person.

5. What is the role of past guilt in our lives?

6. Was Melissa right to consider placing her child for adoption? Should she have gone through with the adoption? Why or why not?

7. What was the nature of Melissa's guilt and fear? Have you experienced similar emotions? How?

8. At what point did you see Melissa beginning to behave as a mature adult? How did that manifest itself?

Now that Jeremy Hamilton has returned to
Davis Landing, he's ready to discover his place
in the world. But is love in God's plan for Jeremy?
Find out in CHRISTMAS HOMECOMING
by Lenora Worth,
coming in December 2006
from Steeple Hill Love Inspired.

Gabi Valencia stopped, her heart picking up its pace as she saw him. She took a second glance, just to make sure. It was *him* all right. The man she'd talked to two days ago in the day care room of the church. He'd just gotten out of an expensive sedan, and he was walking up to the church with some of the Hamilton clan.

He sure cleans up nicely, Gabi thought as she took in the tall man dressed in a tailored overcoat and dark wool suit. His outfit probably cost more than one of her weekly paychecks could cover, she decided, wondering who this man really was.

He looked up then, his eyes locking with hers. At first, he seemed apprehensive and unsure, but then he sent her a hesitant smile, and he kept looking until Gabi felt a tug on her coat.

"Mom?"

Gabi glanced down at Talia. "What, honey?"

"Inside, remember? You wanted to get inside."

"Right, so I did." Gabi dropped her gaze, then turned to find her friend Dawn Leroux coming toward her.

"Dawn, hi! I tried to call you the other night. I wanted to talk to you about *him*. Only I didn't know that he was…well, *him*, then." She lifted her head toward the stranger. "You weren't home."

And now she wished she'd left a message. But Gabi had decided that Dawn's not being home had to be a sign to drop the whole thing. She had no business asking questions about a handsome stranger, especially since the stranger was obviously a friend of the Hamiltons. Way out of her league.

Dawn glanced in the direction of Gabi's gaze. "Oh, *him*. I wanted to talk to you about him, too," Dawn said, her tone a bit too smug, her blue eyes bright with hope. "He does have a striking presence, doesn't he?" Then as if realizing what Gabi had said, she asked, "What about him?"

"I've met him," Gabi whispered as they walked into church. "He was painting in the day care the other day."

"Really? That's great," Dawn said, grinning. "I convinced him to help out. Oh, I'm so glad he actually took my advice."

Realization flared through Gabi. "*That's* the man you told me about—the man who left town because of a personal crisis?"

"That's him," Dawn said. "My future brother-in-law, Jeremy Hamilton."

Jeremy Hamilton. He seemed so different from all the rest. Of course, if the rumors were true—he was different.

They found a pew and both women sank down, the girls settling beside Gabi. Her mouth fell open as she turned to whisper to Dawn. "He's a Hamilton? You sure didn't mention that," she said, her gaze scanning the church doors for any sign of the topic of conversation.

Gabi quickly turned face forward as Jeremy entered with his brother Tim. Suddenly all the pieces began to fall into place. This sure explained his almost aloof behavior the other day when she'd stumbled upon him painting. The man had every reason to be aloof. The Hamiltons were the local dynasty in these parts. Upper crust and top shelf, and all over the local tabloid newspaper. She couldn't believe she hadn't at least recognized him that day. But she'd never mingled in the same social circles as Jeremy Hamilton.

"I can't believe you didn't tell me," she whispered to Dawn.

Dawn glanced down at the church bulletin, then frowned. "But I did. I told you all about him."

Leaning close, Gabi replied, "You just said you had a friend who'd been going through a rough time and needed some space, so you suggested he volunteer at the church." Then she brought a hand to her mouth. "He's the older brother. The one who—"

Dawn interrupted with a whispered sigh. "He's still a Hamilton, no matter who his biological father was. And he's struggling, Gabi. With so many things. Jeremy and Tim have been at odds for a long time, but Tim wants to make amends. Jeremy is still hurting, though, and he needs to feel the love and trust of his church home—that's why I suggested he volunteer here."

Gabi lowered her head. It was so like gentle Dawn to figure out a way to put Jeremy at ease, and to bring him back to his faith. "I understand that, but you could have warned *me*. I actually flirted with the man!"

Dawn lifted an eyebrow, then smiled. "I didn't tell

you his name because I didn't want to gossip in detail about his personal problems," she said, glancing back to wave to other church members. "And I didn't know he'd show up at the church so quickly." Then she grinned again. "And I certainly didn't plan on you running into him there, even though that worked out perfectly, if you ask me."

"What do you mean?" Gabi said, careful to keep her voice low. All around them, people were greeting each other and laughing and talking. It was always like this before the service began.

Dawn shot her another hopeful glance. "Oh, nothing. Just…well…he's lonely, Gabi. He needs a friend. And you're—"

"A single *mother*," Gabi reminded her, her eyes going wide as she emphasized that fact. "A single mother from the wrong side of the tracks. And he's the CEO of Hamilton Media. Dawn Leroux, are you trying to set me up with Jeremy Hamilton?"

"Maybe," Dawn replied. "And he's not the CEO these days. But I'm hoping we can work on that, too." Then her smile widened as her fiancé, Tim Hamilton, came up the aisle and sat down beside her.

Gabi spoke to Tim, then stared ahead, listening while Dawn and Tim whispered and cooed to each other, their newfound love endearing and sweet. Then she felt Dawn's arm on hers.

"Scoot over."

Gabi glanced up as she moved down the aisle to make room. She knew who it would be, waiting to take a seat at the end of the pew. Jeremy Hamilton looked at her, waved a hand, then sat down, his head turned toward her. He mouthed a "Hi, there," his eyes moving over Gabi and her girls.

Gabi gave him a weak smile, then turned to fuss over Talia and Roni as the organ music indicated the start of the service.

"Who is that, Mommy?" Roni asked, leaning forward to peer down the aisle.

"Just a friend," Gabi said, pushing her inquisitive daughter back against the pew. "Don't stare, honey. It's impolite."

"Well, he keeps staring at *us*," Talia pointed out, waving at Jeremy.

He waved back. And finally cracked a smile.

"He's just being friendly," Gabi said. Then she handed her daughter crayons and a fresh sheet of notepaper from her purse. "Draw me a picture."

As the choir began singing the intro, Gabi stole another glance down the aisle herself. Jeremy Hamilton was indeed smiling at her. And that smile sent a warm thrill all the way down to Gabi's black leather ankle boots.

Oh, Lord, she began to pray. *I'm sure in trouble here. Please help me to put this man out of my mind. Let me be a friend to him, to minister Your tender mercies, nothing more.*

But that particular prayer seemed to go unheard. Because all during the service, Jeremy Hamilton was front and center in Gabi's thoughts, and for more reasons than just tender mercies.

Love Inspired

CHRISTMAS HOMECOMING

BY
LENORA WORTH

Davis Landing

**Nothing is stronger
than a family's love.**

After leaving town to
meet the grandparents
he'd never known about,
Jeremy Hamilton returned
to Davis Landing. He
wasn't ready to embrace
his own father, but found
himself drawn to single
mother Gabi Valencia. Would
her charm and spirituality
help create a Christmas
homecoming for Jeremy?

**Steeple
Hill®**

www.SteepleHill.com

*Available December 2006,
wherever you buy books.*

LICHLW

REQUEST YOUR FREE BOOKS!

2 FREE INSPIRATIONAL NOVELS
PLUS 2
FREE
MYSTERY GIFTS

Love Inspired®

YES! Please send me 2 FREE Love Inspired® novels and my 2 FREE mystery gifts. After receiving them, if I don't wish to receive any more books, I can return the shipping statement marked "cancel." If I don't cancel, I will receive 4 brand-new novels every month and be billed just $3.99 per book in the U.S., or $4.74 per book in Canada, plus 25¢ shipping and handling per book and applicable taxes, if any*. That's a savings of at least 20% off the cover price! I understand that accepting the 2 free books and gifts places me under no obligation to buy anything. I can always return a shipment and cancel at any time. Even if I never buy another book from Steeple Hill, the two free books and gifts are mine to keep forever.

113 IDN EF26 313 IDN EF27

Name	(PLEASE PRINT)	
Address		Apt.
City	State/Prov.	Zip/Postal Code

Signature (if under 18, a parent or guardian must sign)

Order online at www.LoveInspiredBooks.com

Or mail to Steeple Hill Reader Service™:

IN U.S.A.
P.O. Box 1867
Buffalo, NY
14240-1867

IN CANADA
P.O. Box 609
Fort Erie, Ontario
L2A 5X3

Not valid to current Love Inspired subscribers.

Want to try two free books from another series?
Call 1-800-873-8635 or visit www.morefreebooks.com

* Terms and prices subject to change without notice. NY residents add applicable sales tax. Canadian residents will be charged applicable provincial taxes and GST. This offer is limited to one order per household. All orders subject to approval. Credit or debit balances in a customer's account(s) may be offset by any other outstanding balance owed by or to the customer. Please allow 4 to 6 weeks for delivery.

LIREG06

TITLES AVAILABLE NEXT MONTH

Don't miss these four stories in December

LASSO HER HEART by Anna Schmidt

Bethany Taft thought her happiness was gone forever when
her fiancé was killed. But her aunt found love at sixty, offering
Bethany a glimpse of hope—and the chance to spend time with
the groom's handsome son.

CHRISTMAS HOMECOMING by Lenora Worth
Davis Landing

Jeremy Hamilton left town after discovering that he was not his
father's son. Now he's back...in the company of single-mother
Gabi Valencia. Perhaps, spending time with her could lead to
some new family ties for the former business tycoon.

A SEASON FOR GRACE by Linda Goodnight
The Brothers' Bond

The moment they met, social worker Mia Carano knew Officer
Collin Grace was the perfect mentor for a runaway teen in her
care. After all, breaking through his gruff exterior would fulfill a
boy's Christmas wish...and maybe even her own....

LOVE WALKED IN by Merrillee Whren

Getting close to neighbor Clay Reynolds was not a consideration
for Beth Carlson. The single mom had her hands full with her
troubled teen and had no time for romance—especially not with
another motorcycle-riding man.

LICNM1106